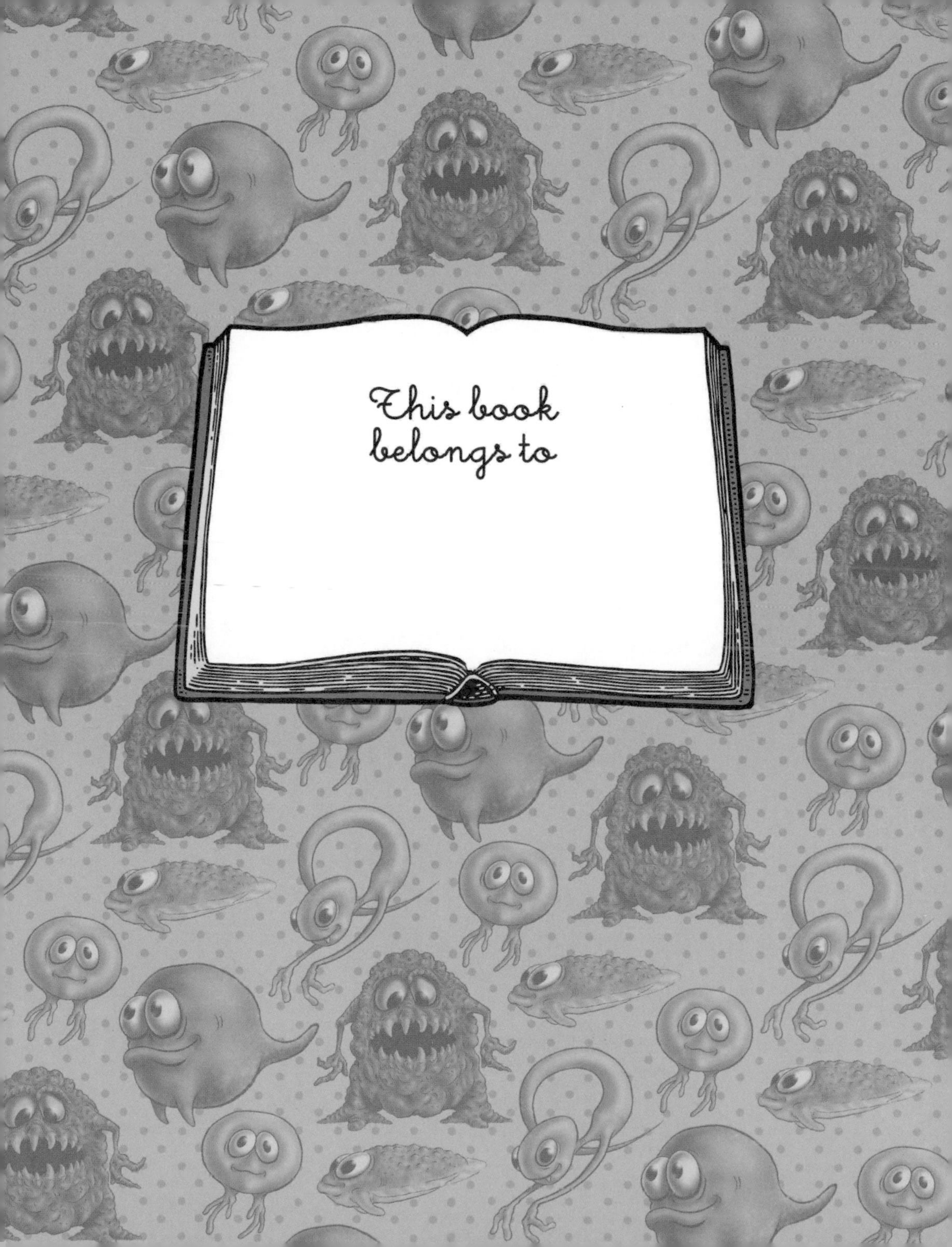
This book
belongs to

DYNAMITE®

Presents

Erf

Written by

Garth Ennis

Illustrated by

Rob Steen

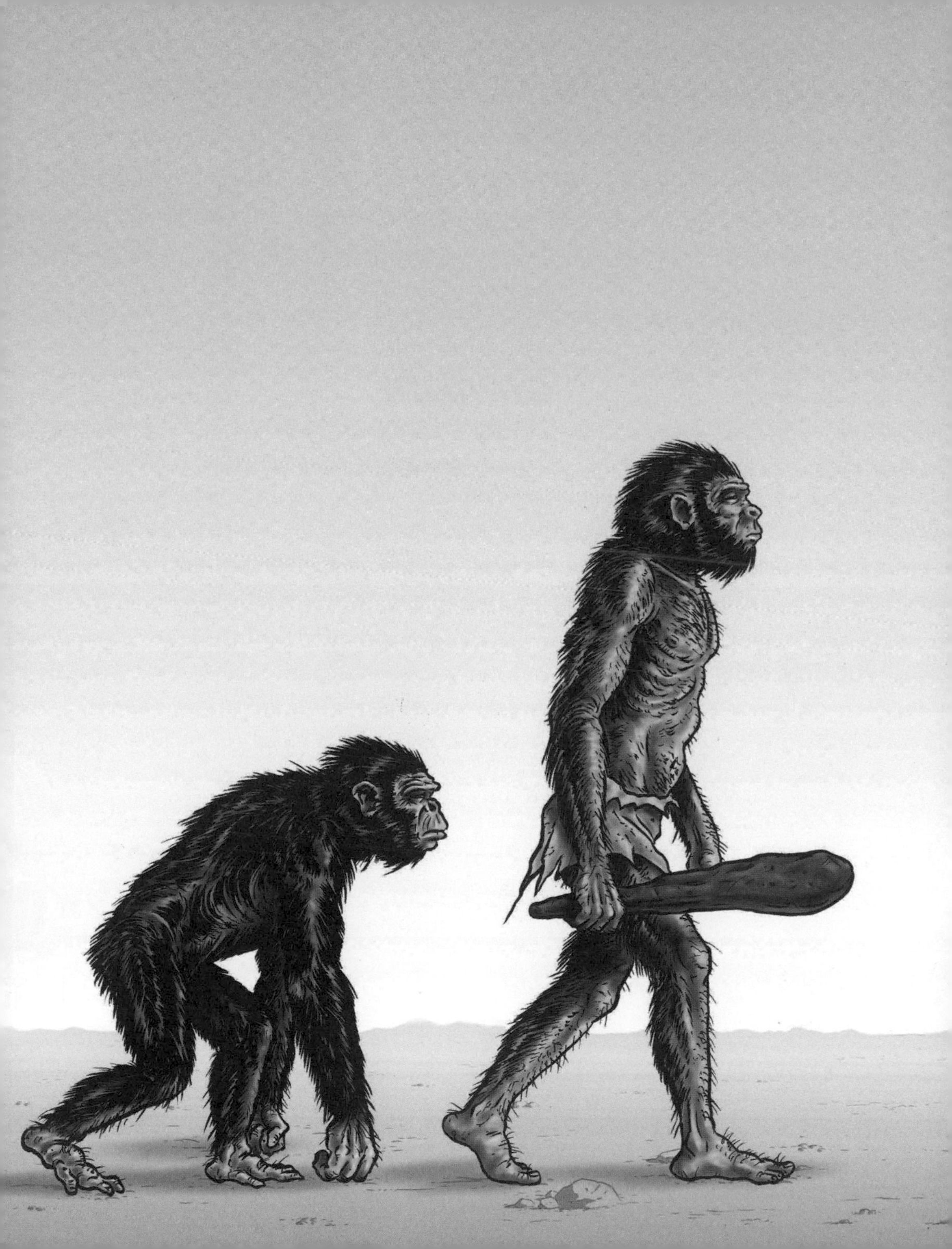

DYNAMITE.

Nick Barrucci, CEO / Publisher
Juan Collado, President / COO
Brandon Dante Primavera, V.P. of IT and Operations

Joe Rybandt, Executive Editor
Matt Idelson, Senior Editor
Kevin Ketner, Editor

Geoff Harkins, Creative Director
Cathleen Heard, Senior Graphic Designer
Rachel Kilbury, Digital Multimedia Associate
Alexis Persson, Graphic Designer
Katie Hidalgo, Graphic Designer

Alan Payne, V.P. of Sales and Marketing
Rex Wang, Director of Consumer Sales
Pat O'Connell, Sales Manager
Vincent Faust, Marketing Coordinator

Jay Spence, Director of Product Development
Mariano Nicieza, Director of Research and Development

Amy Jackson, Administrative Coordinator

ISBN13: 978-1-5241-1221-9
First Printing 10 9 8 7 6 5 4 3 2 1

www.DYNAMITE.com | Facebook **/Dynamitecomics** | Instagram **/Dynamitecomics**
Tumblr **dynamitecomics.tumblr.com** | Twitter **@dynamitecomics** | YouTube **/Dynamitecomics**

Erf. First printing. Published by Dynamite Entertainment, 113 Gaither Dr., STE 205, Mt. Laurel, NJ 08054.

Printed in China.

For information regarding press, media rights, foreign rights, licensing, promotions, and advertising e-mail: marketing@dynamite.com

A long, long, long, long, long, long, long, long, LONG time ago, the world was a very different place.

Because the continents that we know were all joined up, or split apart, and the countries that we know hadn't even been heard of yet.

And in those days, everyone lived in the ocean...

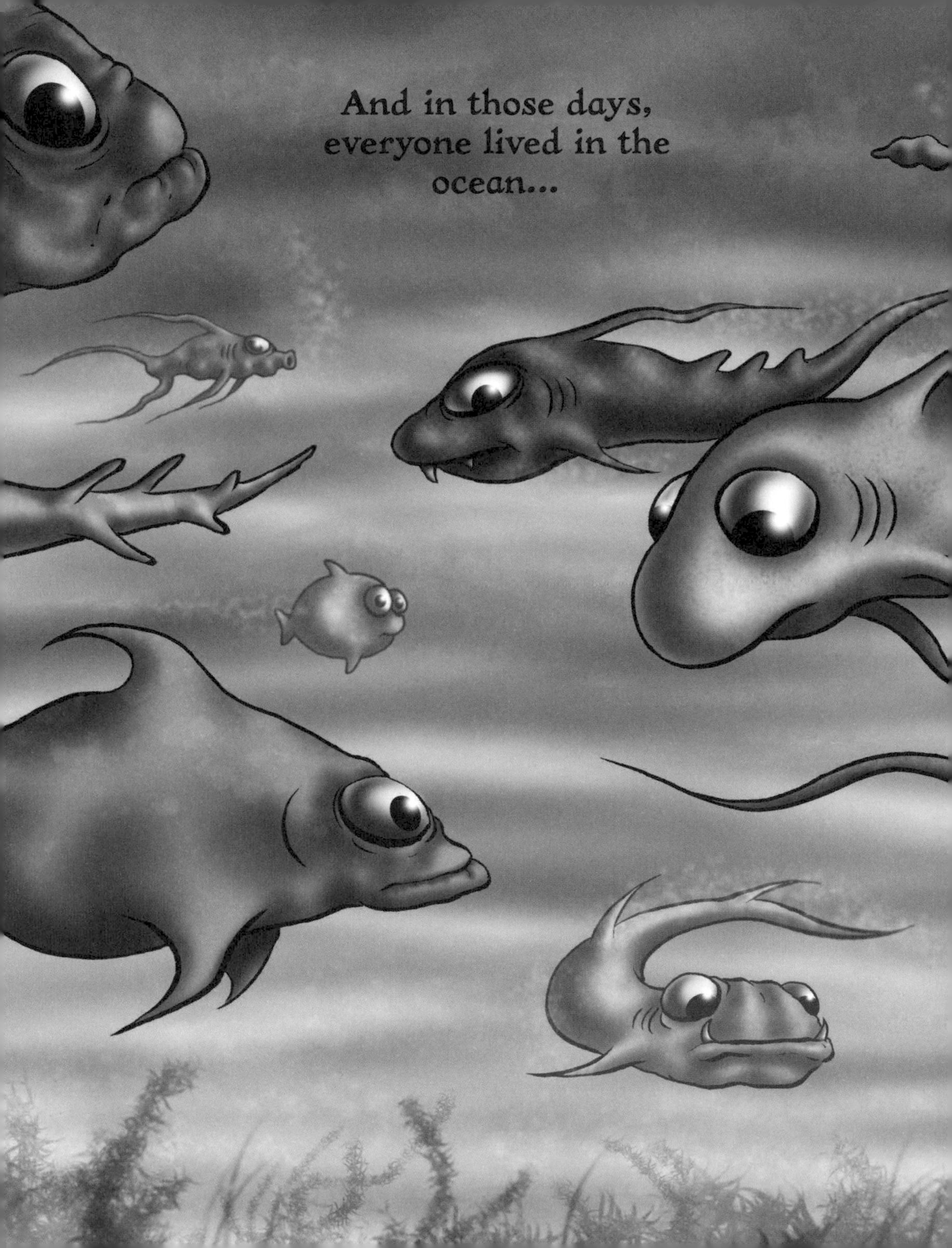

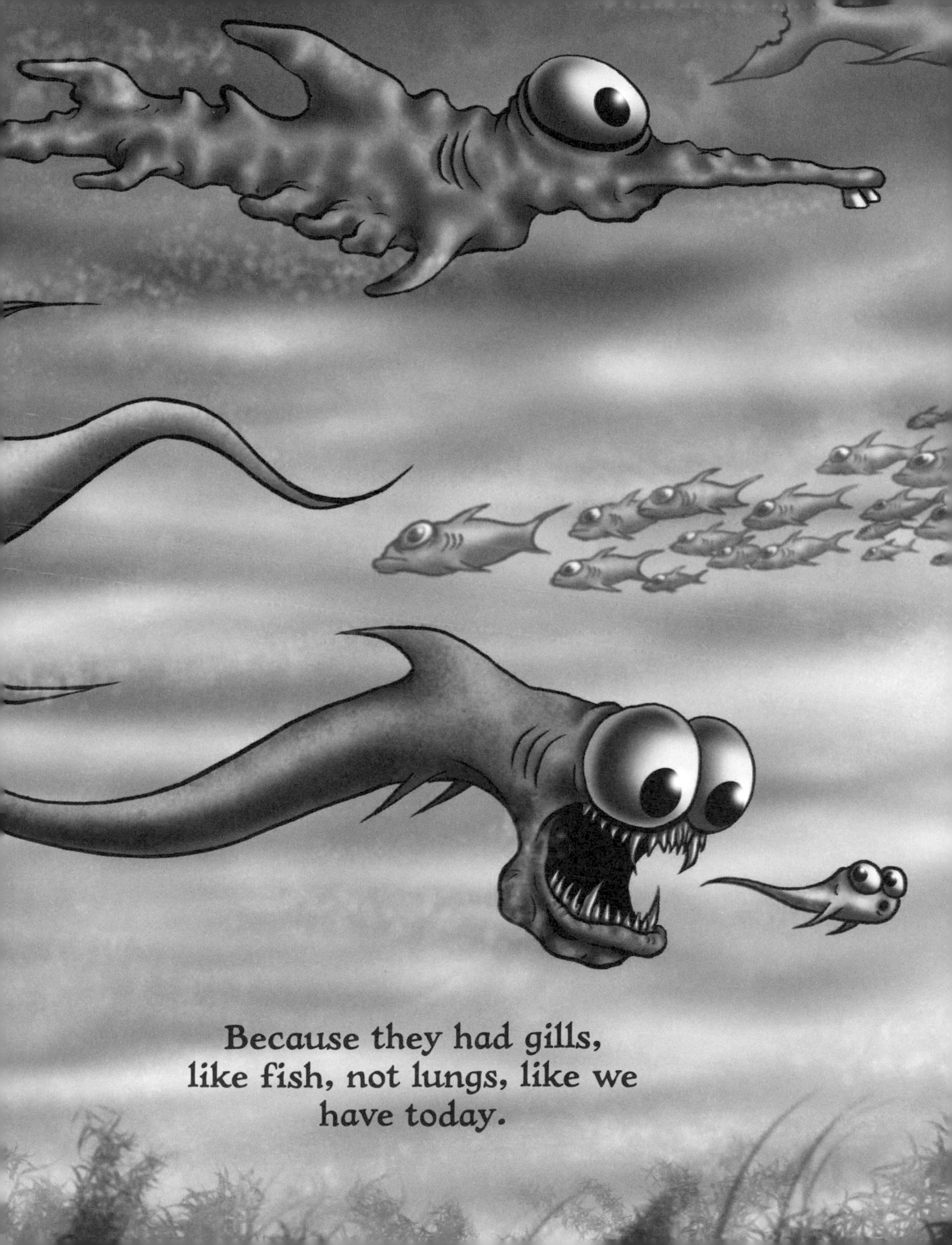

Because they had gills,
like fish, not lungs, like we
have today.

And among all the folk who lived in the sea were four friends:

Figwillop...

The Booper...

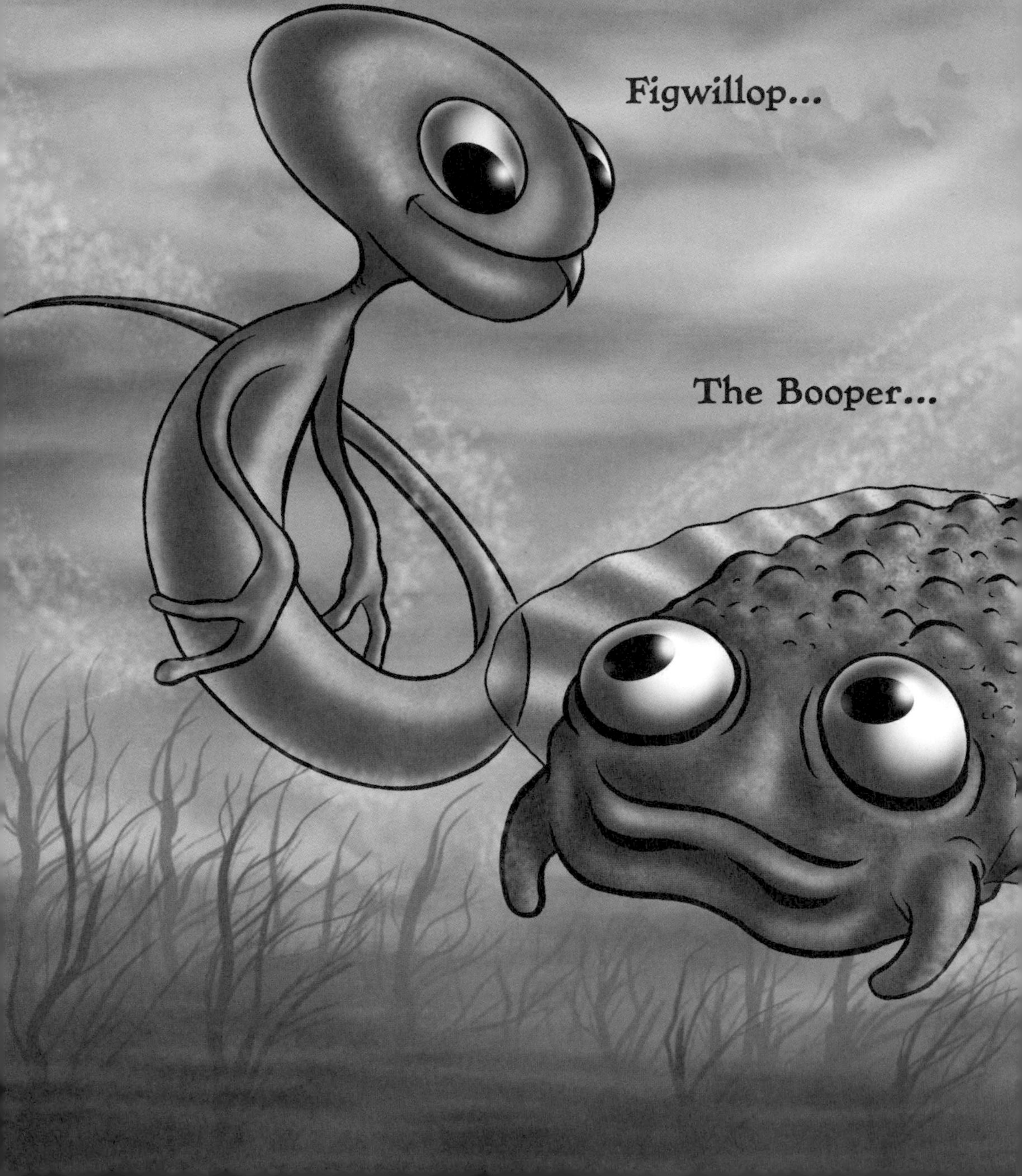

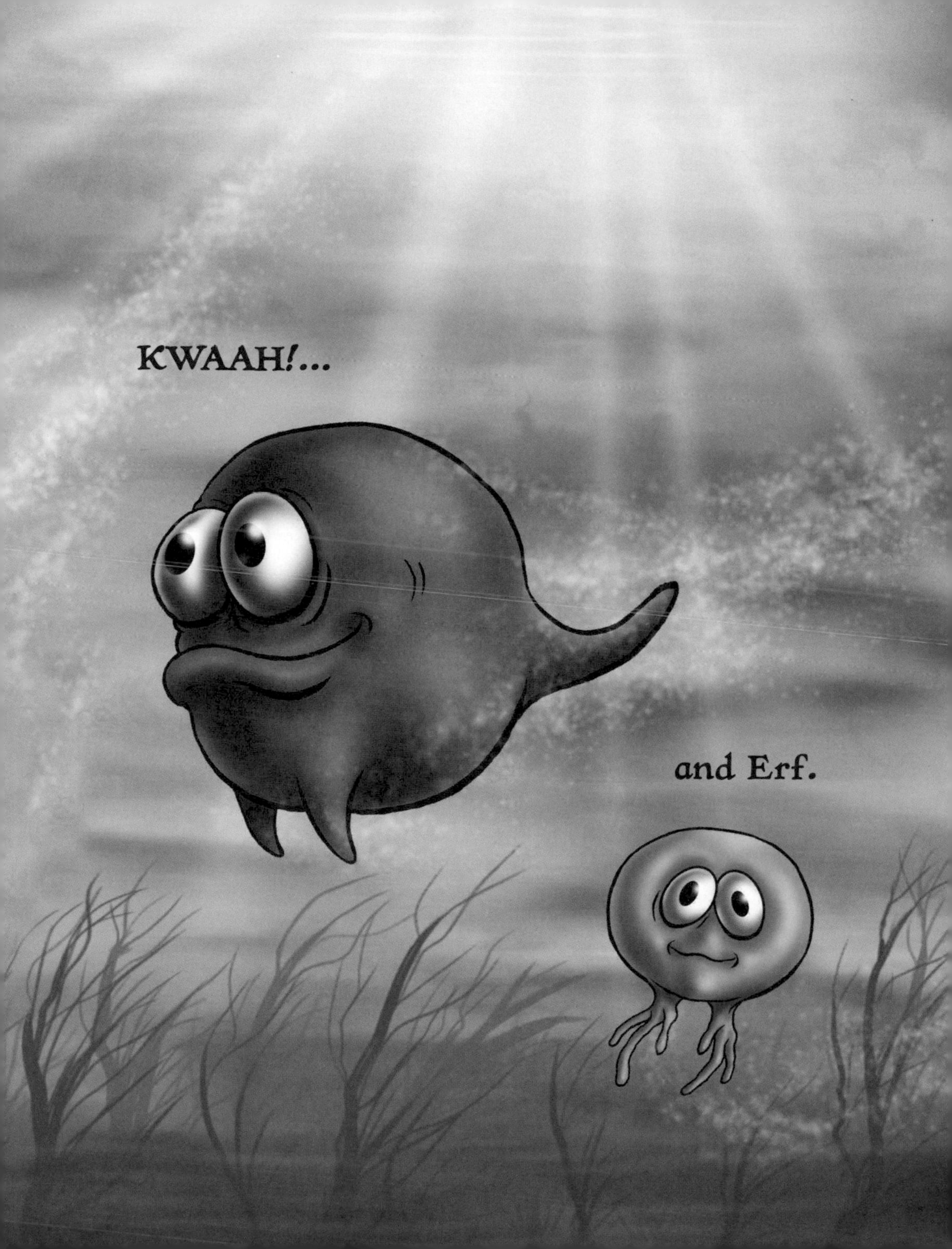

KWAAH!...

and Erf.

Now Figwillop, The Booper, KWAAH! and Erf did everything together ~ even though Erf was not as strong as his friends, and sometimes had a hard time keeping up with them.

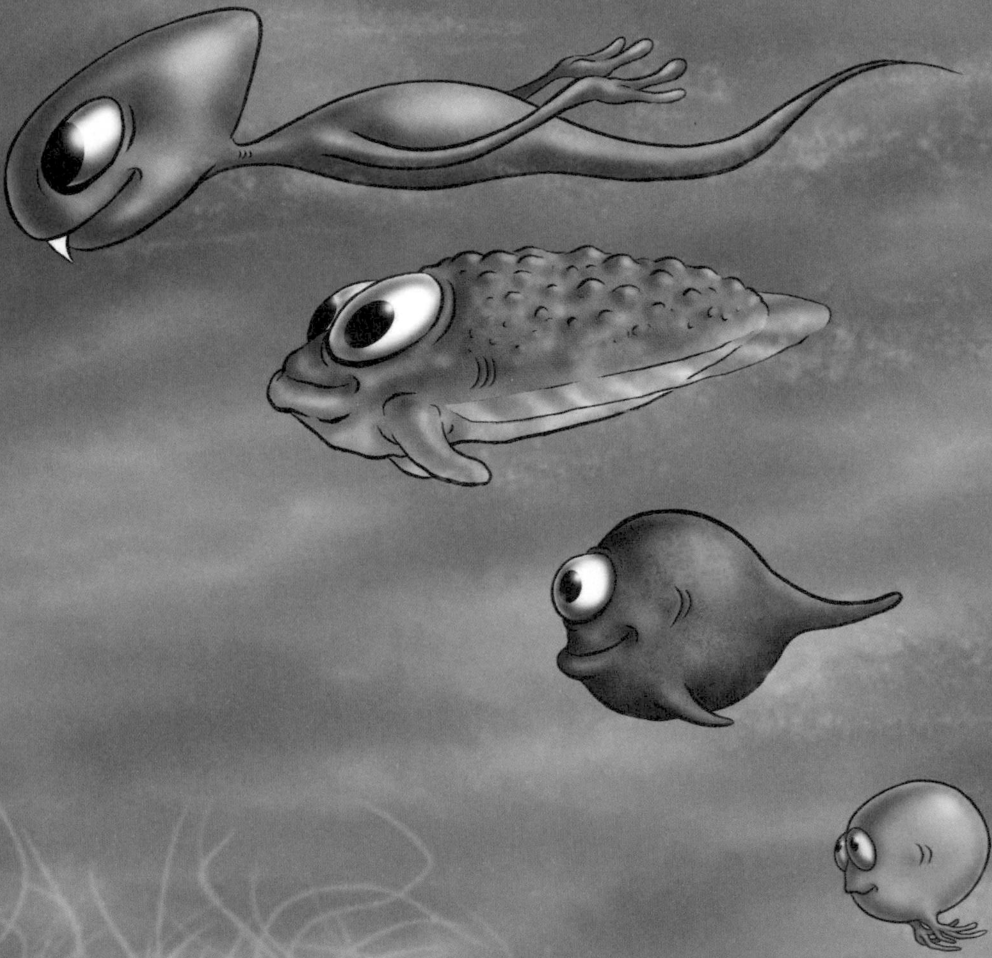

You see, each of his friends had a special talent...

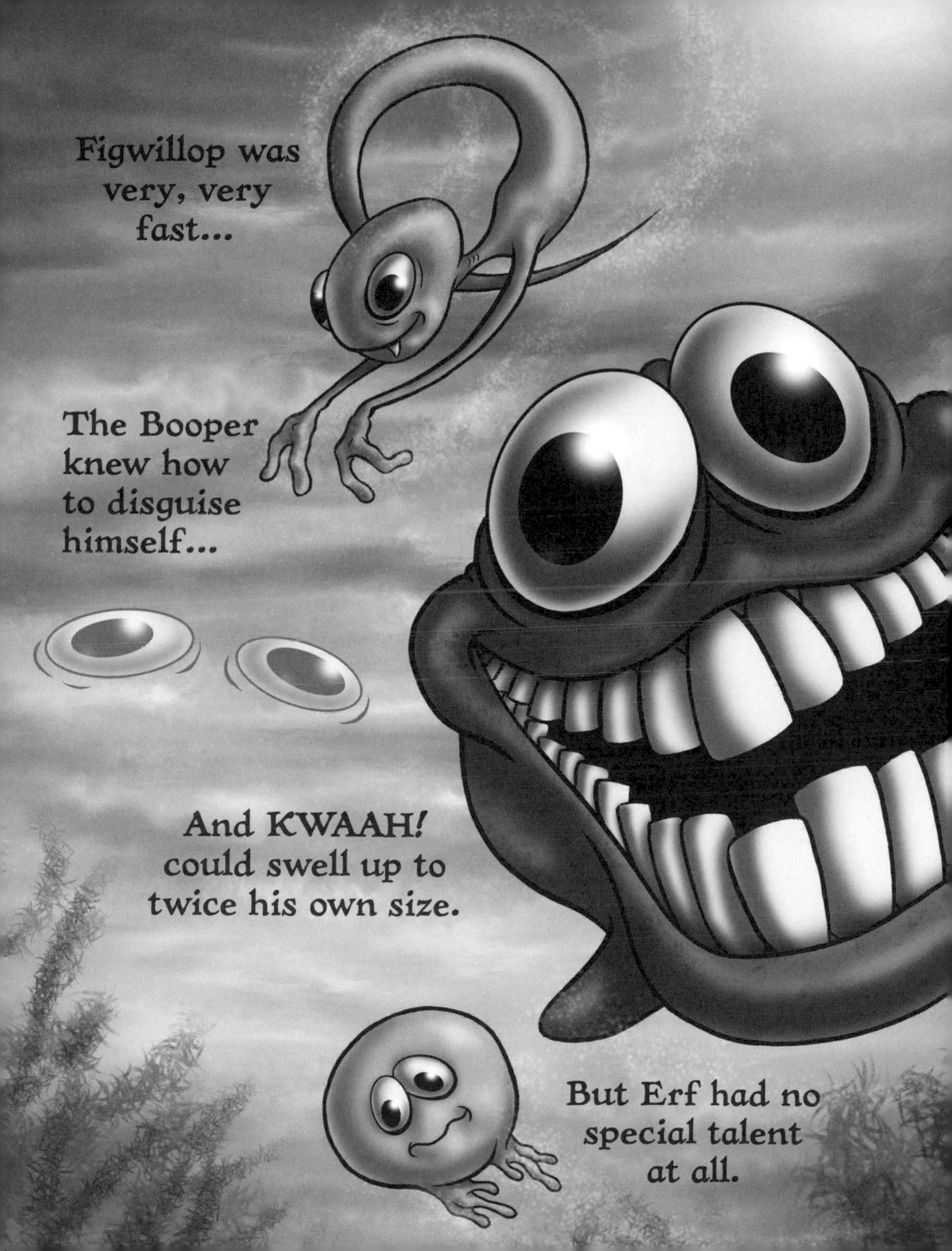

Figwillop was very, very fast...

The Booper knew how to disguise himself...

And KWAAH! could swell up to twice his own size.

But Erf had no special talent at all.

All Erf could do was go...

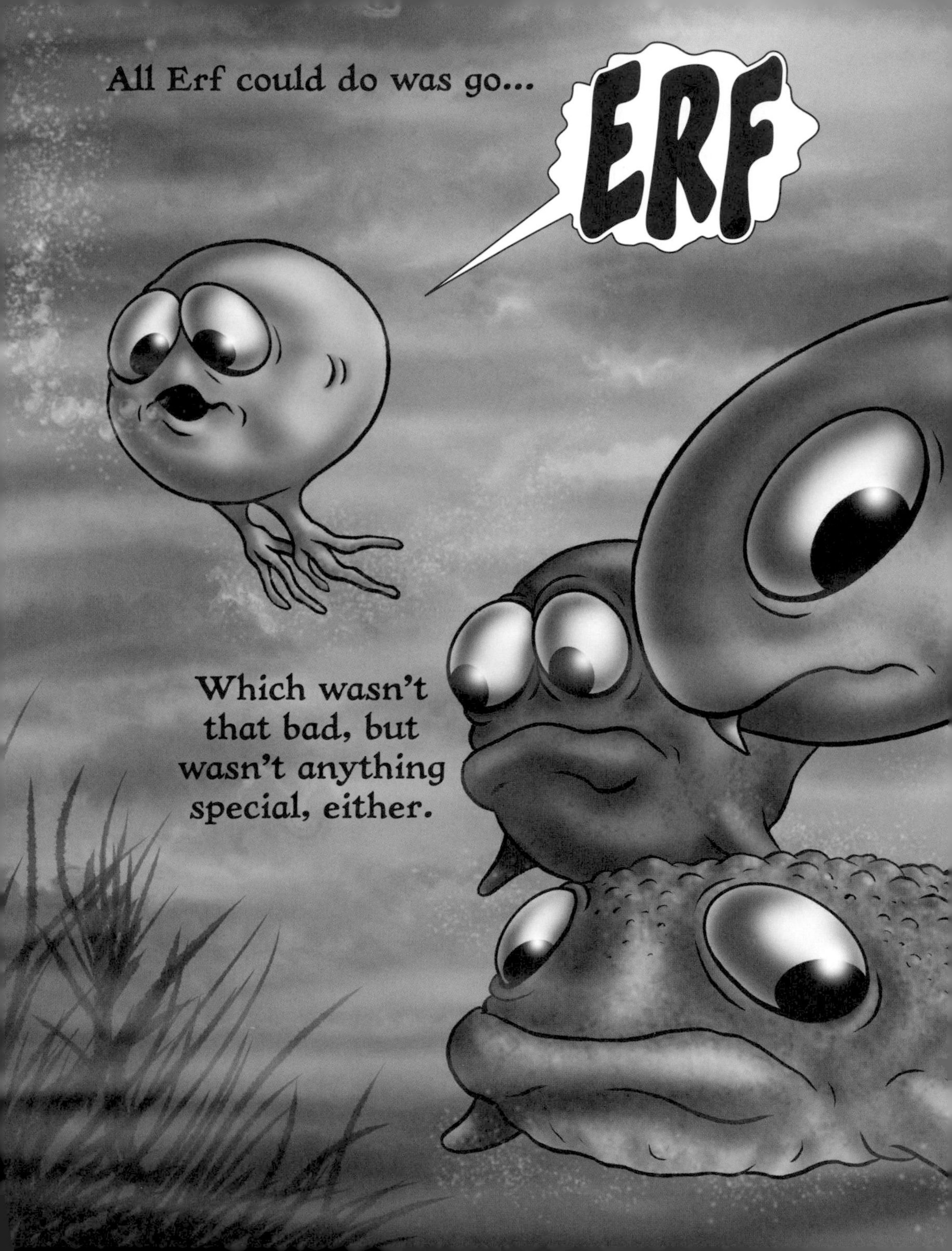
ERF

Which wasn't
that bad, but
wasn't anything
special, either.

All the same, Erf loved his friends.
And they loved him, even if sometimes they
forgot that he had trouble keeping up.

Even if sometimes they forgot to
tell Erf that they loved him.

(Because they had their talents...
and Erf did not.)

And then...
one day...
a strange thing happened.

Figwillop, The Booper, KWAAH!
and Erf poked their noses out of
the water...

And found they could breathe.

Because although they hadn't
known before, they had lungs as
well as gills.

The four friends looked at the world beyond the ocean, a place they'd never even imagined.

It looked very scary off in the distance, with volcanoes exploding, and lava flowing, and clouds of black soot filling the air...

But closer,
they saw a little island~
and it didn't seem very
scary at all.

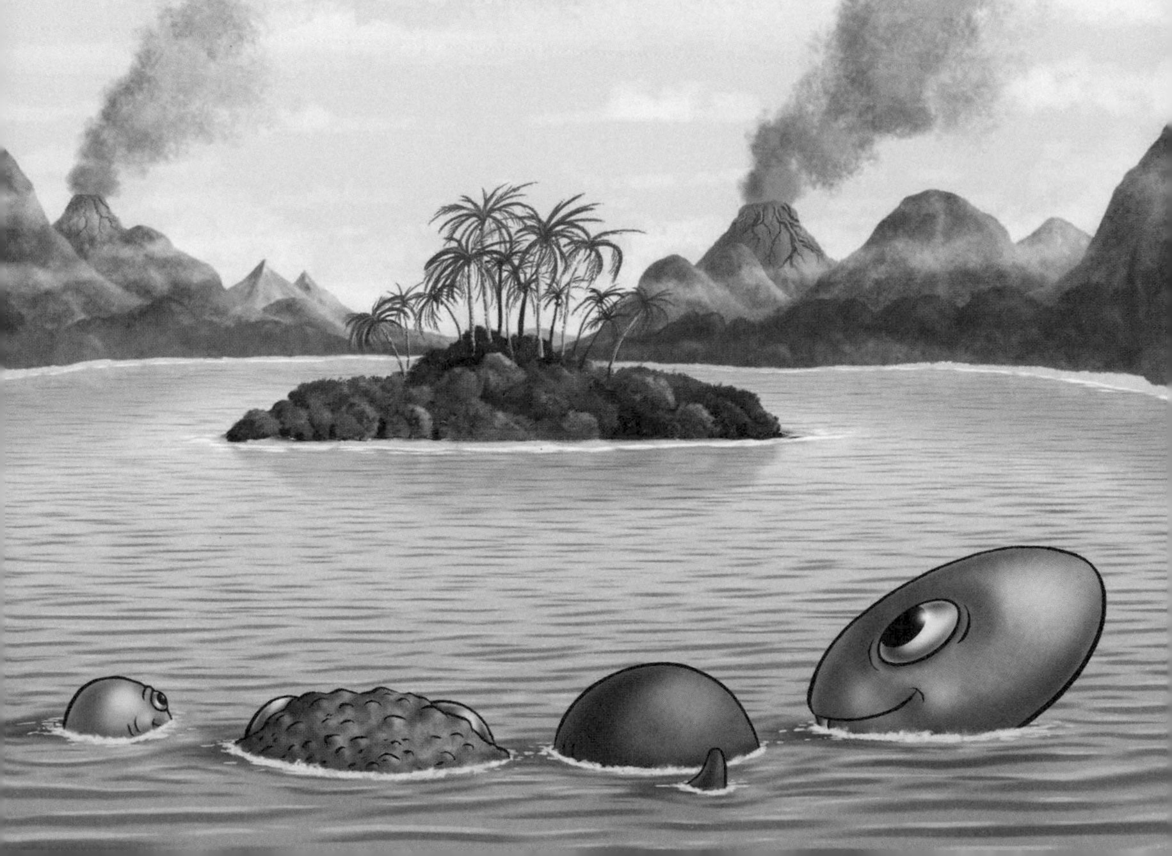

And then they did an incredible thing.

For the first time ever...

They left the water...

And breathed in the air...

And wriggled and
squiggled up onto
the land.

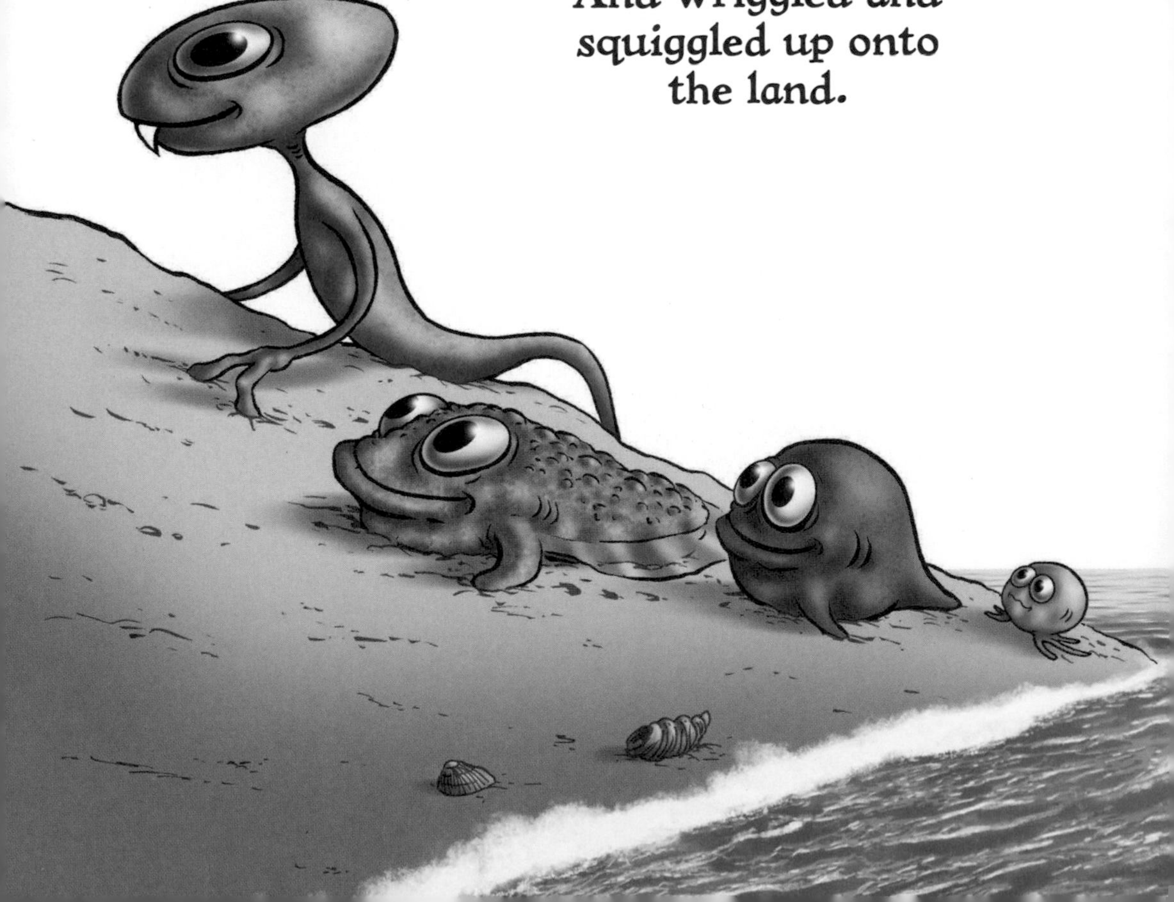

And OH! The fun that they had in their brave new world!

Figwillop rolled in the crunchy sand, and The Booper disguised himself as a plant, and KWAAH! ate berries he found on a bush~

And Erf climbed a tree!

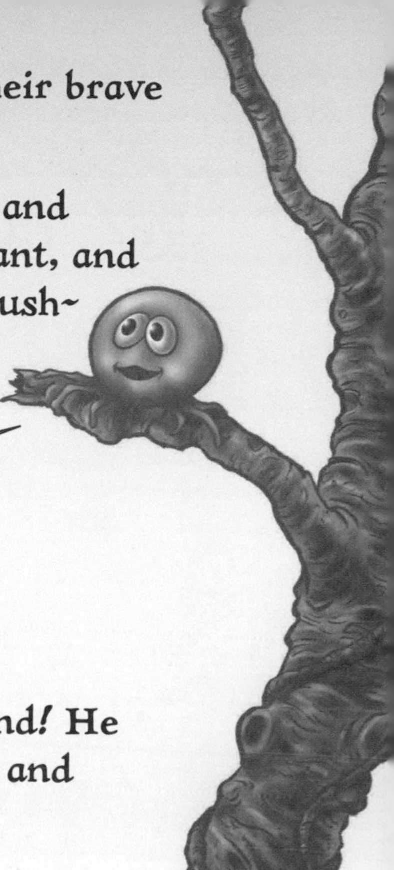
I CAN SEE, I CAN SEE! I CAN SEE, I CAN SEE!

And he saw the ocean! He saw the land! He saw everything that there was to see, and everything that would ever be!

And he saw~

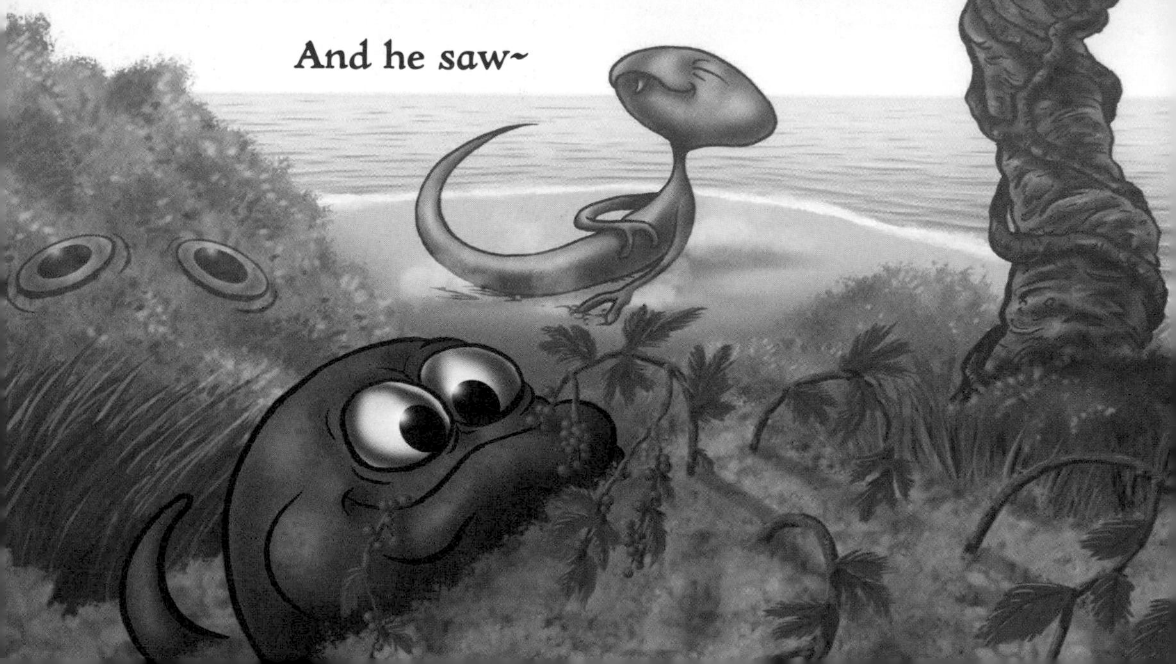

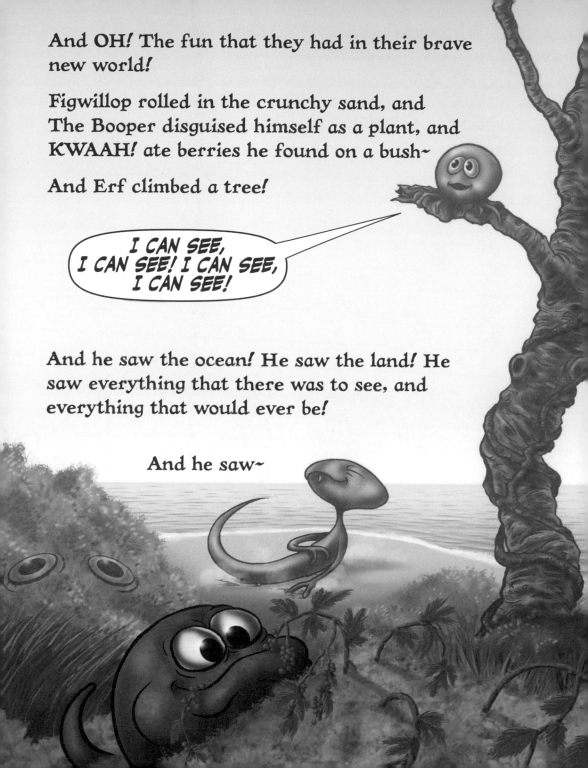

Uh-oh.

Erf had met the

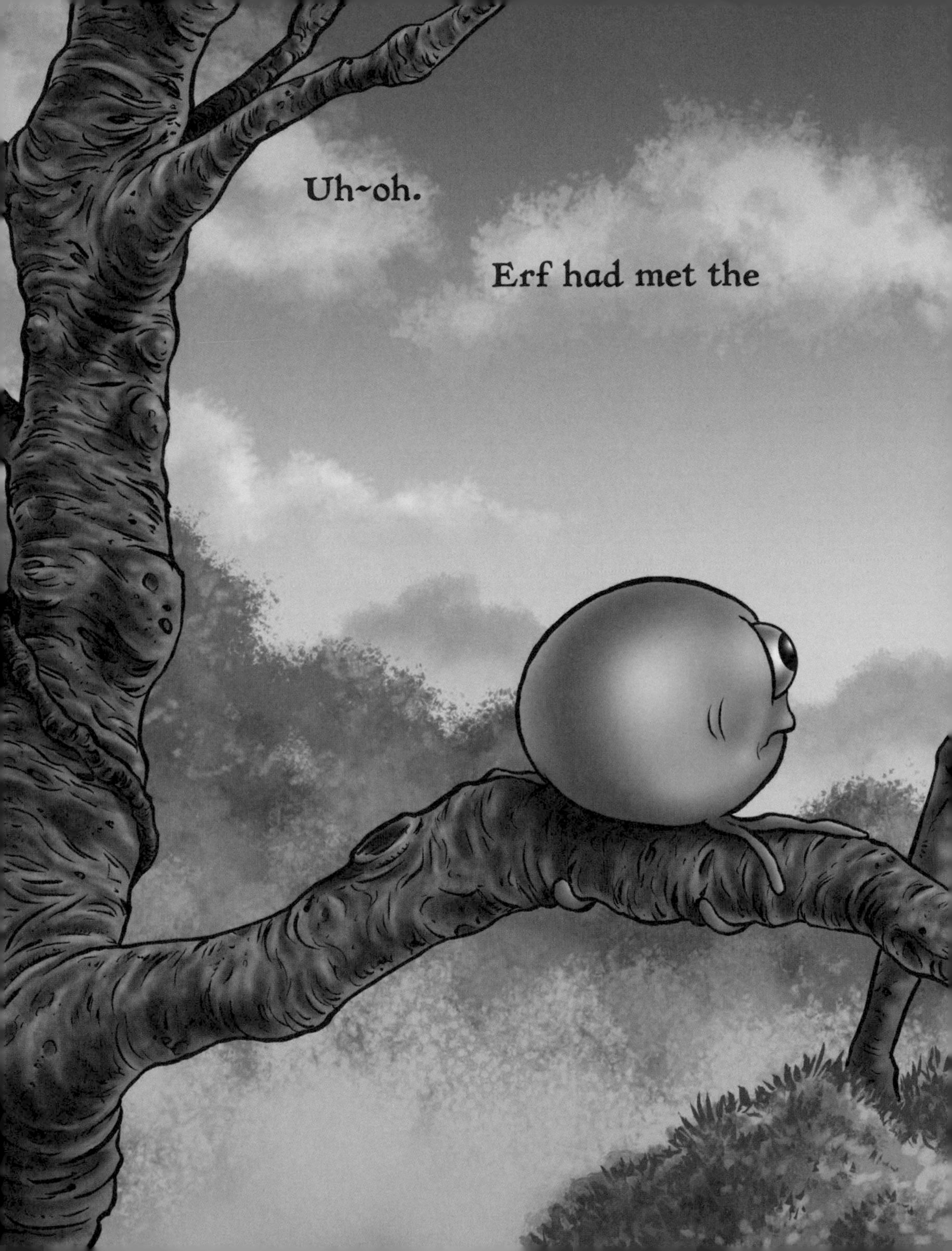

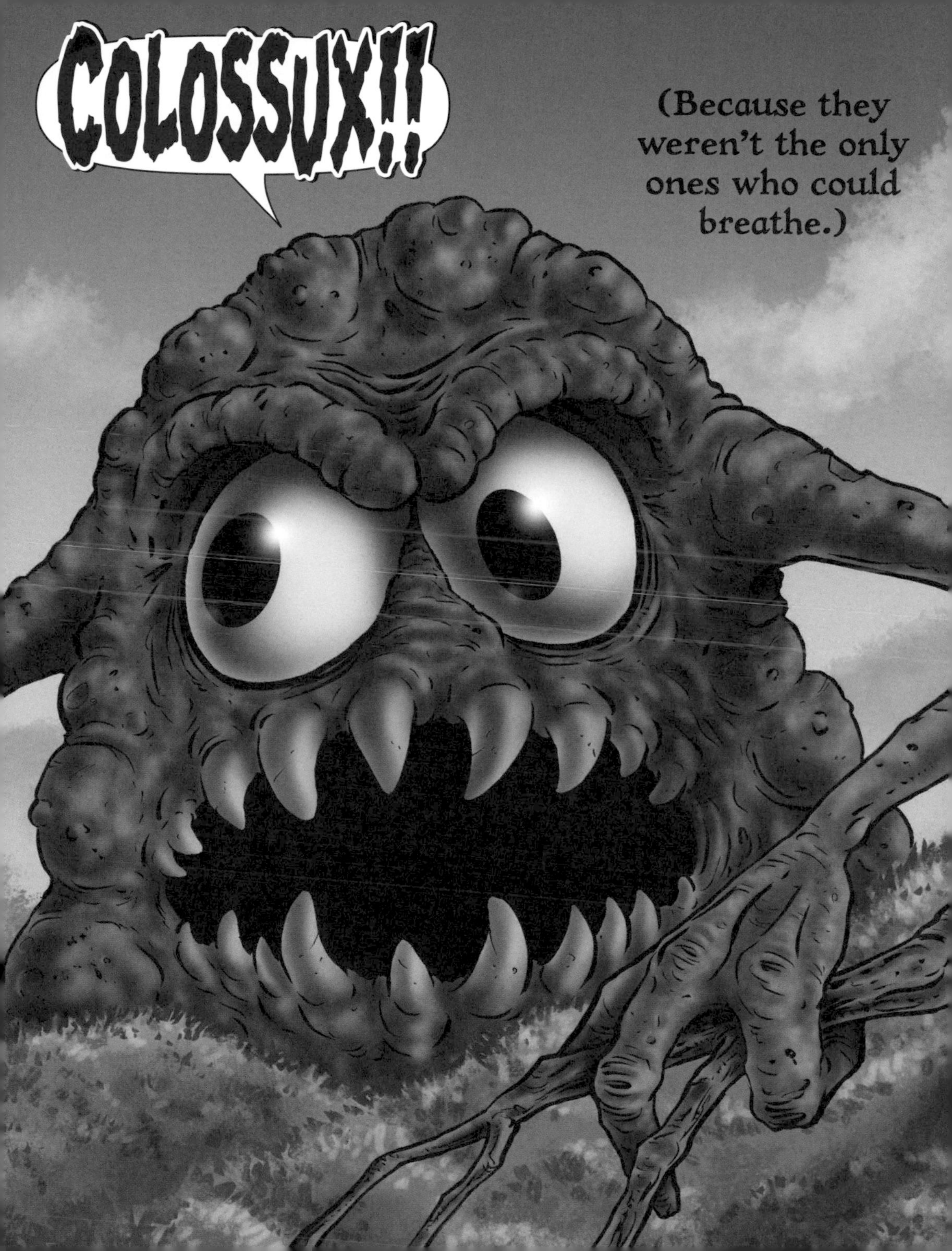
COLOSSUX!!
(Because they weren't the only ones who could breathe.)

"Well, well!" the Colossux said, and the friends were very scared.

"Well, well!" the Colossux said, and they squeaked, "Please, sir!"

"Well, well!" the Colossux said, and they gasped, "We didn't know it was YOUR island!"

"Well, well!" the Colossux said. "It looks like I've found my DINNER!"

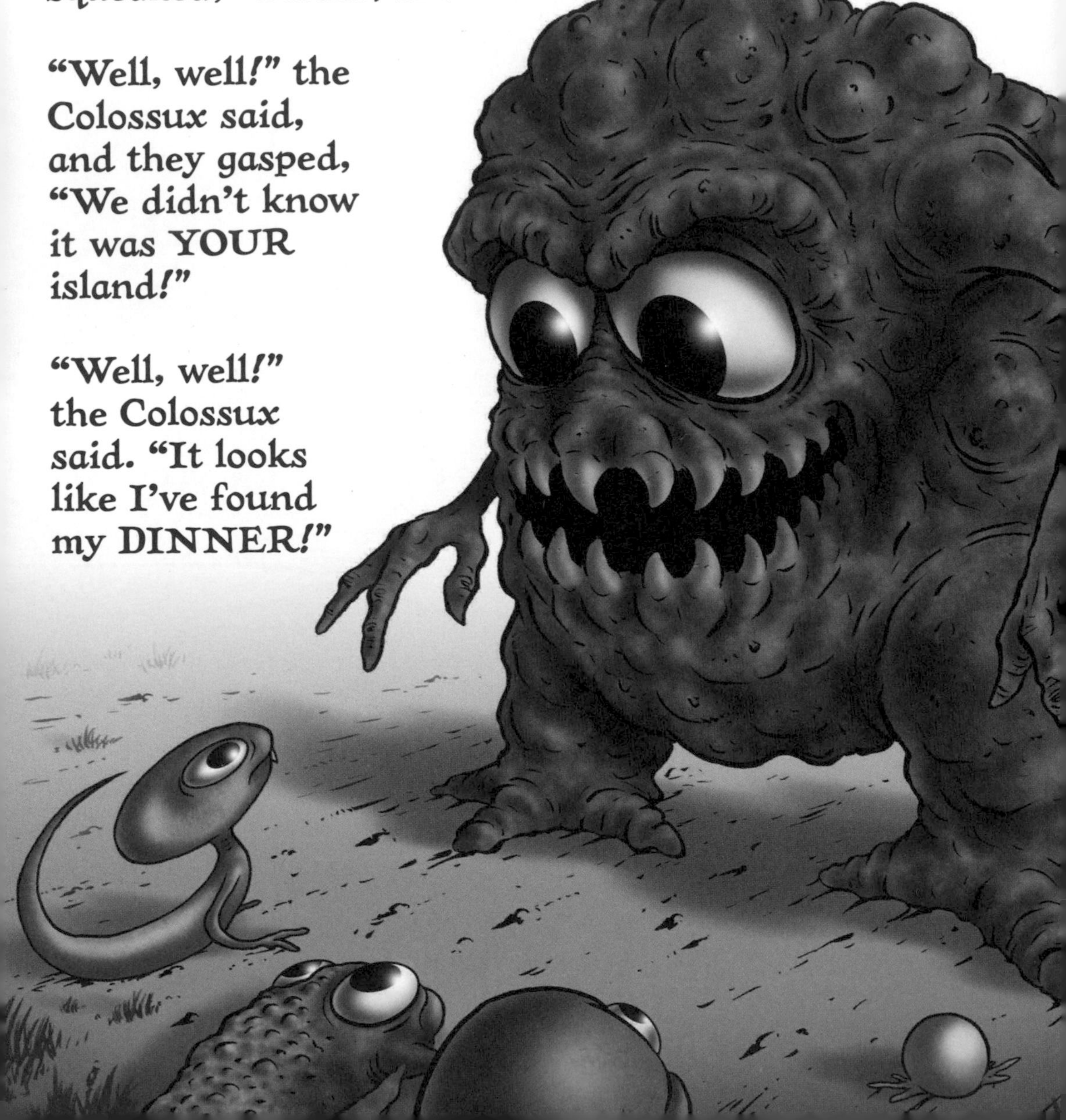

"I am very hungry indeed," he said, "because I need to gather my strength to swim to the mainland. There is much, much more there to do, and much, much more to eat."

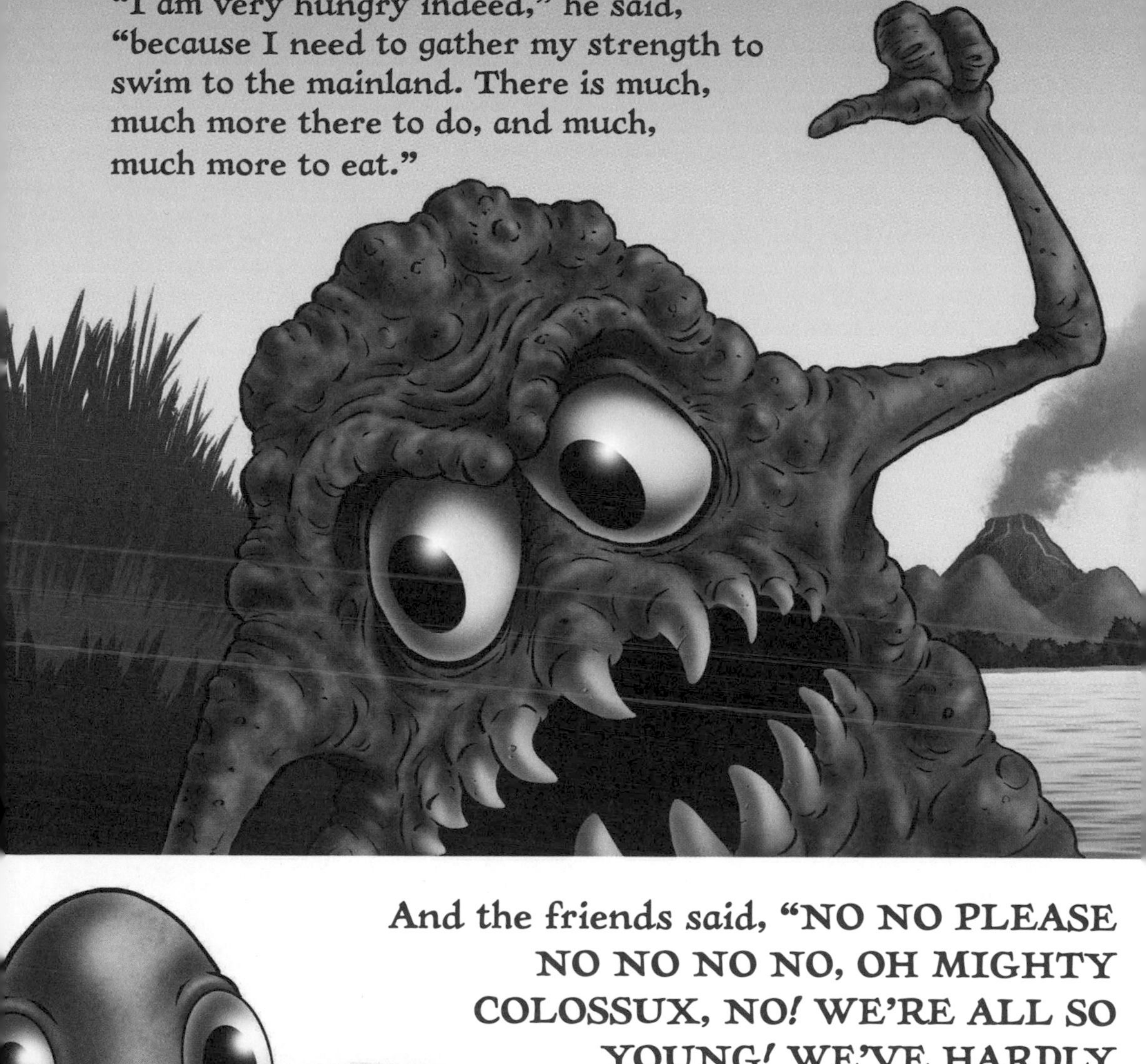

And the friends said, "NO NO PLEASE NO NO NO NO, OH MIGHTY COLOSSUX, NO! WE'RE ALL SO YOUNG! WE'VE HARDLY LIVED! DON'T EAT US FOR DINNER, PLEASE!"

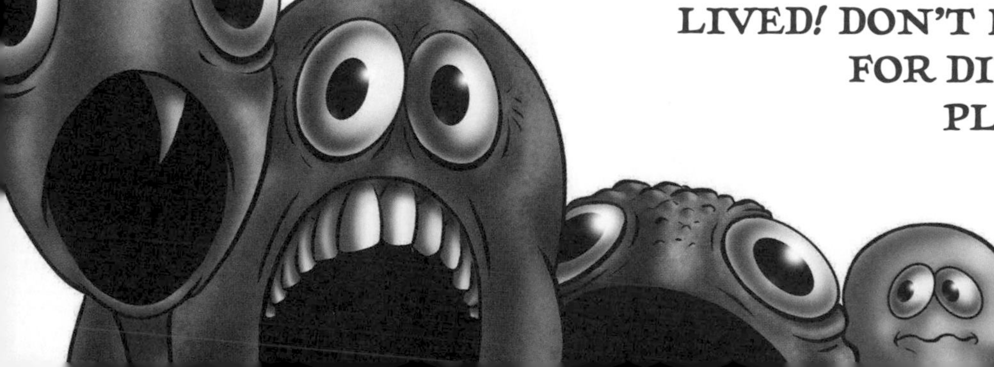

"Well..." said the Colossux...

"WELL..."

(And the friends were very tense.)

"I suppose it isn't that far to swim. I suppose I only need one of you.

"So here is what I will do: I will give you until tomorrow morning to decide who I will eat. Then I will be on my way, and the other three will never have to worry about me again.

"BUT...

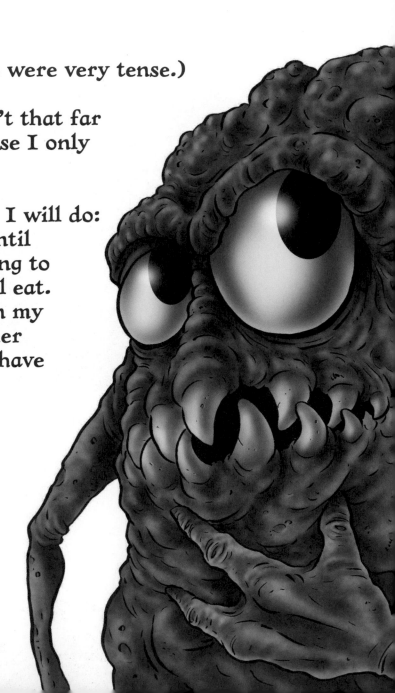

"Don't even THINK about escape."

"Because I am much, much faster than you," he told Figwillop.

"And I can smell anyone in disguise," he told The Booper.

"And I can eat anyone twice your size," he told KWAAH!

"And I can... yes, well, anyway," he told Erf.

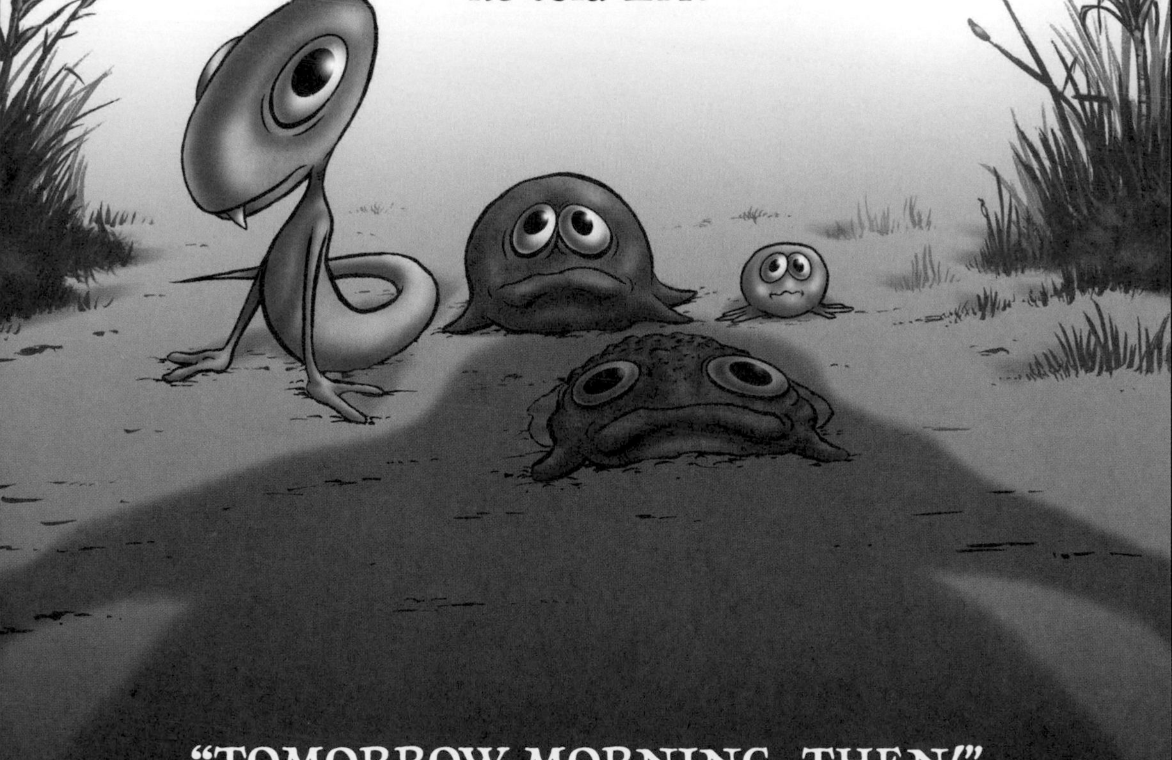

"TOMORROW MORNING, THEN!"

And with that, he went off to enjoy a nap.

The friends were silent for a while.
Then Figwillop said...

"I really am quite fast, you know. That's quite a talent. I don't think I should be the one to be eaten."

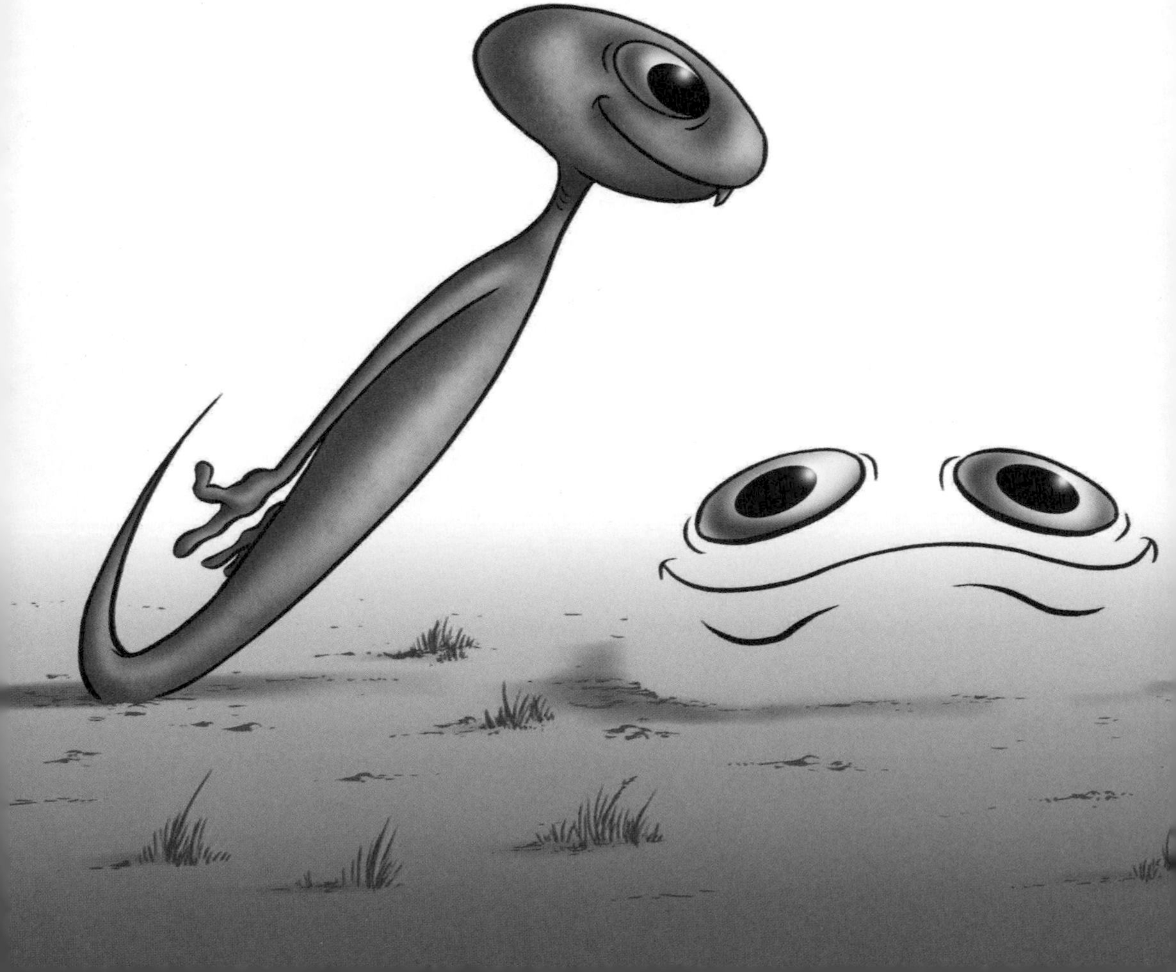

And The Booper said,
"My disguise is very clever. I don't think it should be me."

And KWAAH! said,
"I can swell up to twice my size. It definitely shouldn't be me."

And Erf said—

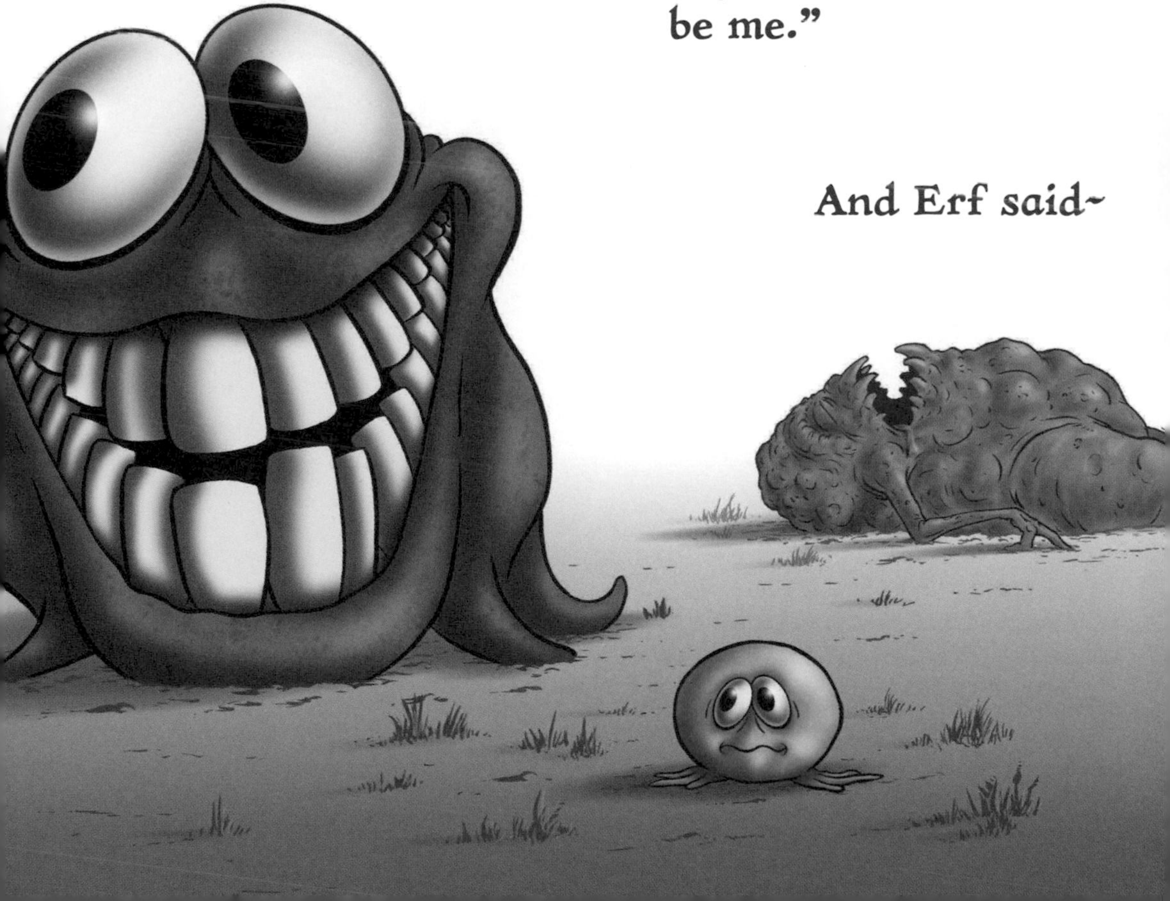

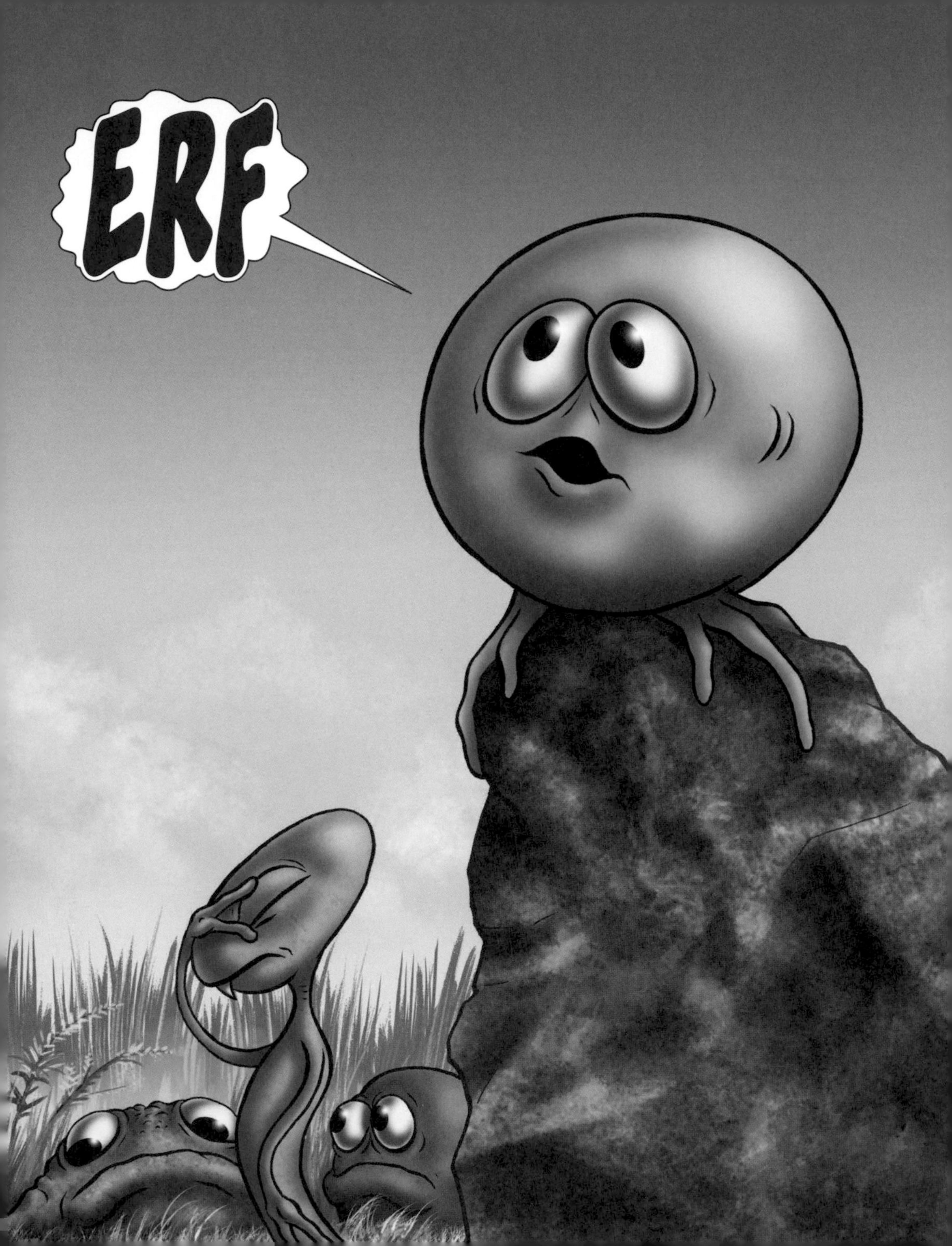
ERF

“Well...” said Figwillop,
“I suppose we don’t have to
decide now...”

“Yes,” said The Booper,
“we can make up our minds in
the morning, can’t we?”

“Then one of us,”
said KWAAH! “can go and
see the Colossux.”

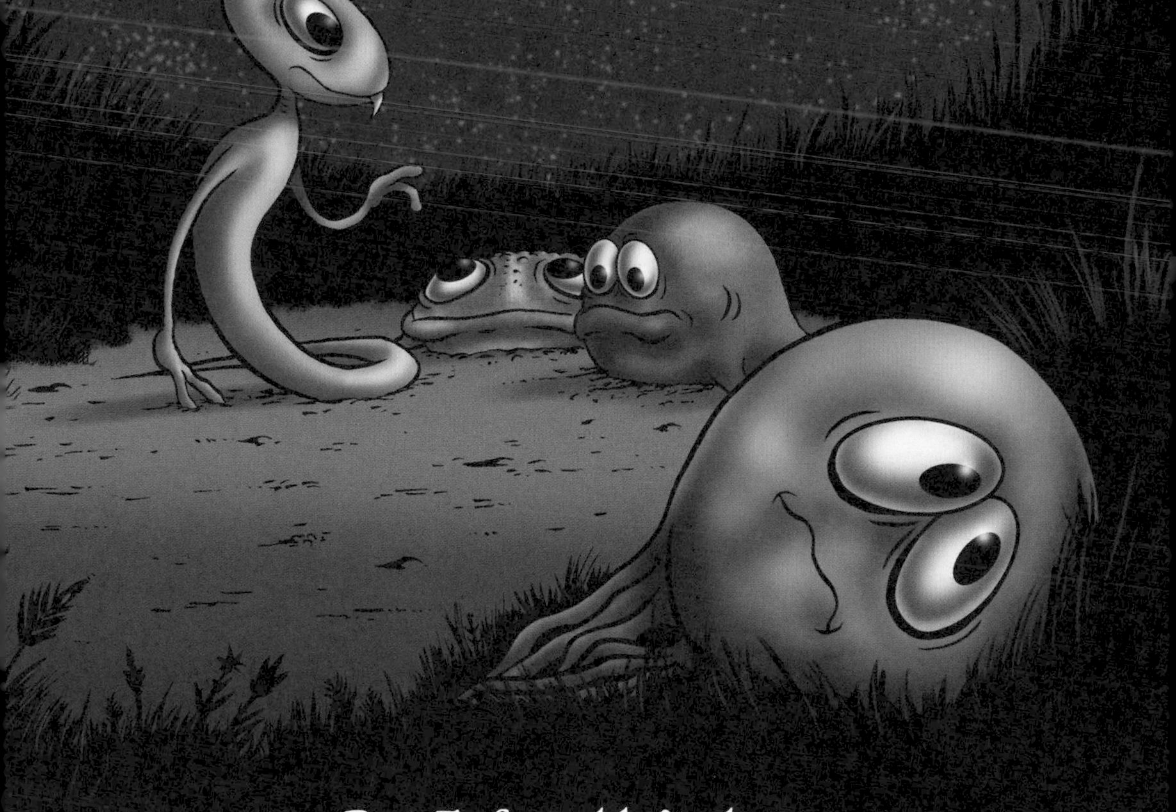

But Erf couldn’t sleep.

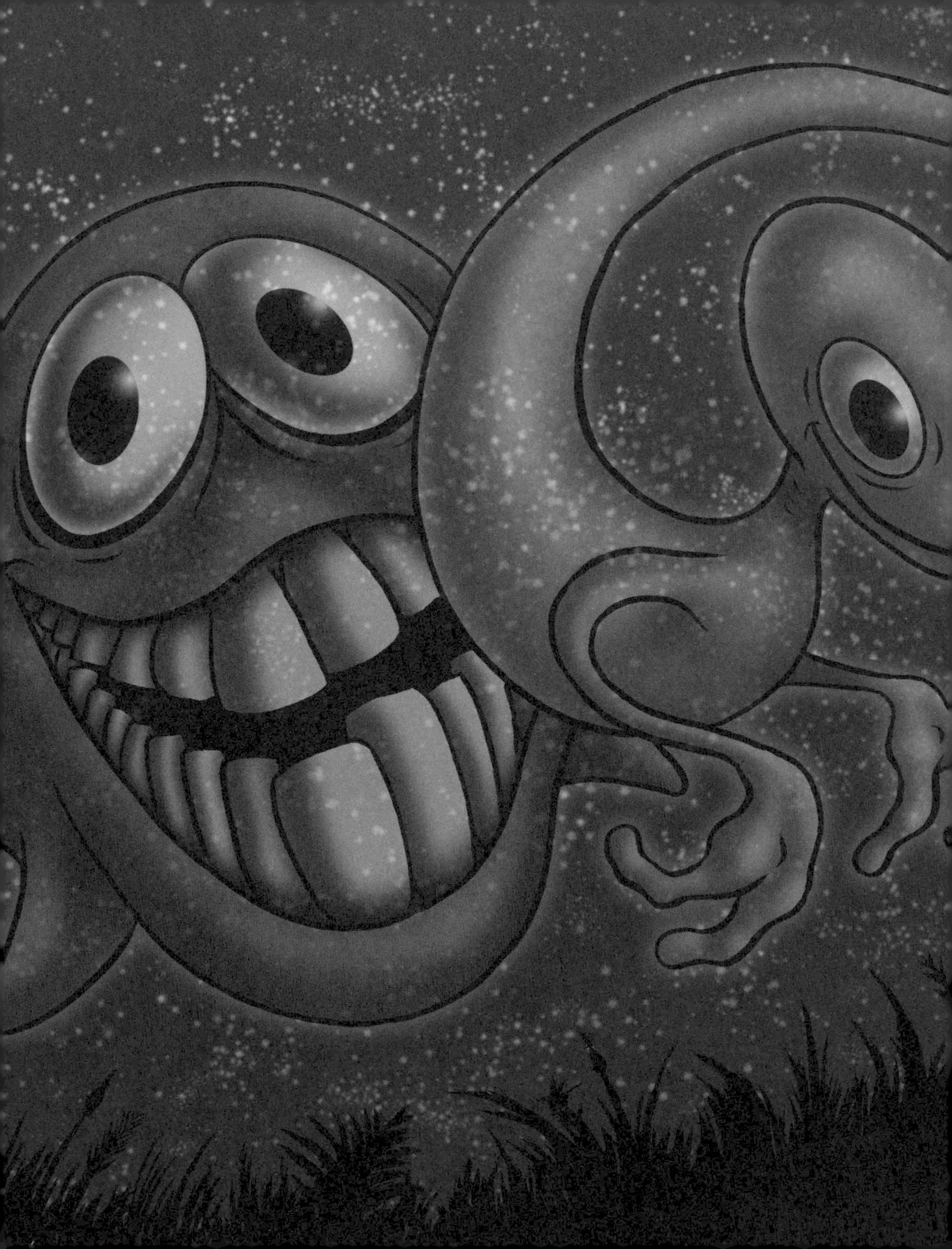

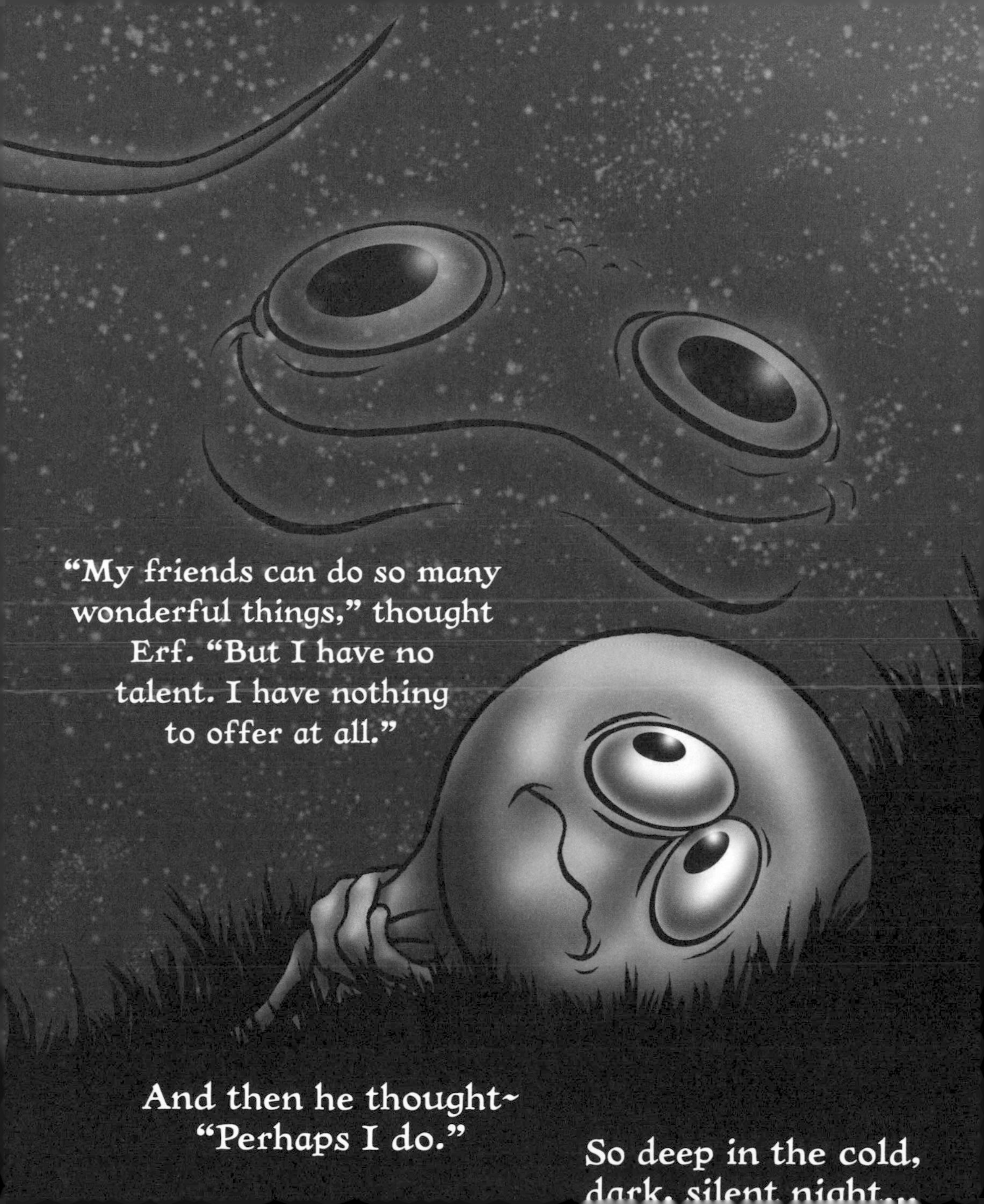

"My friends can do so many wonderful things," thought Erf. "But I have no talent. I have nothing to offer at all."

And then he thought~
"Perhaps I do."

So deep in the cold,
dark, silent night…

Erf went to see the Colossux.

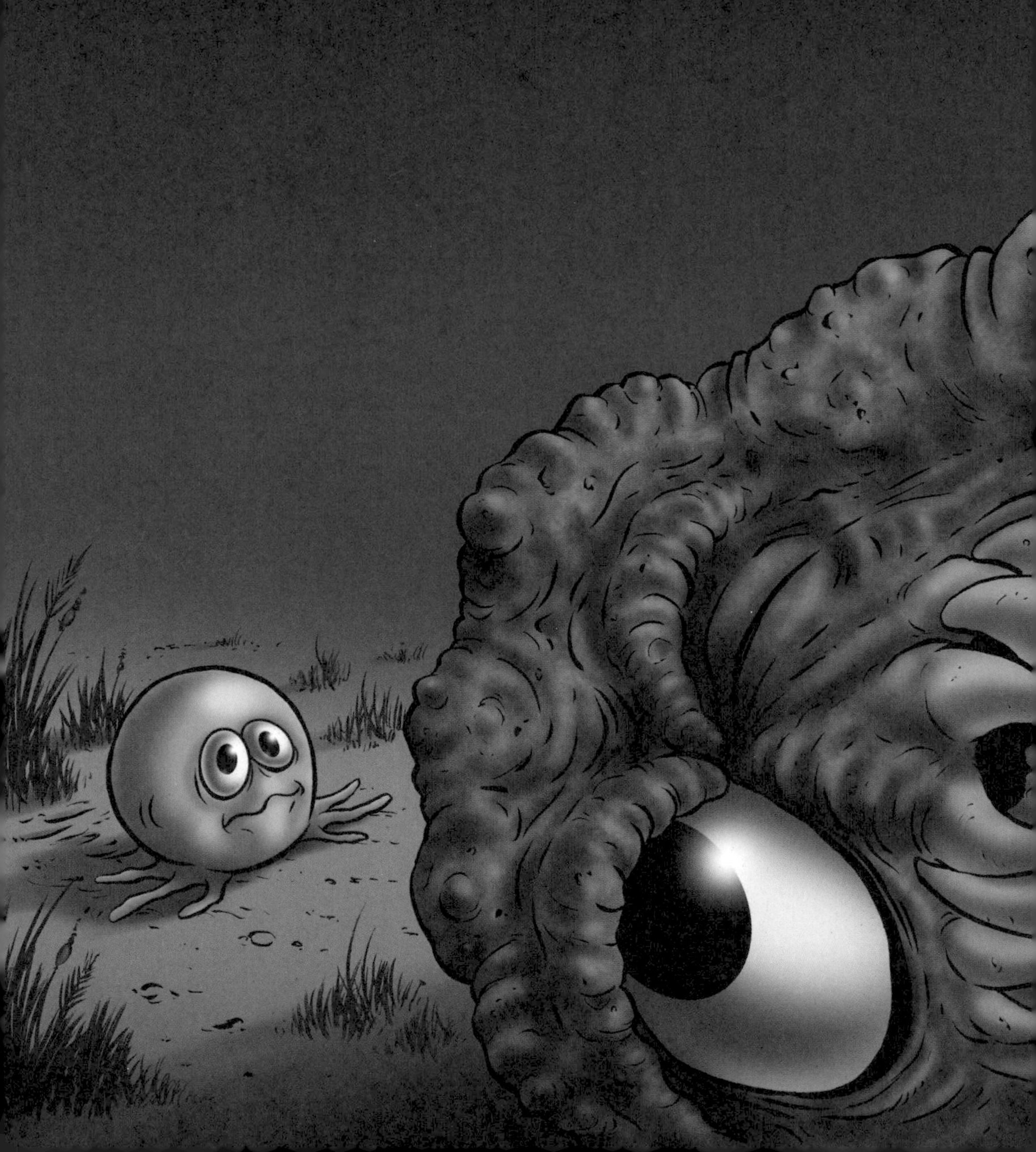

"So it is to be you," the Colossux said.
"That's what has been decided?"

"Yes," said Erf, "it's been decided.
Do you promise to leave my friends alone?"

"I do," said the Colossux. "I shall go on
my way, as good as my word."

"Then," said Erf, "so be it."

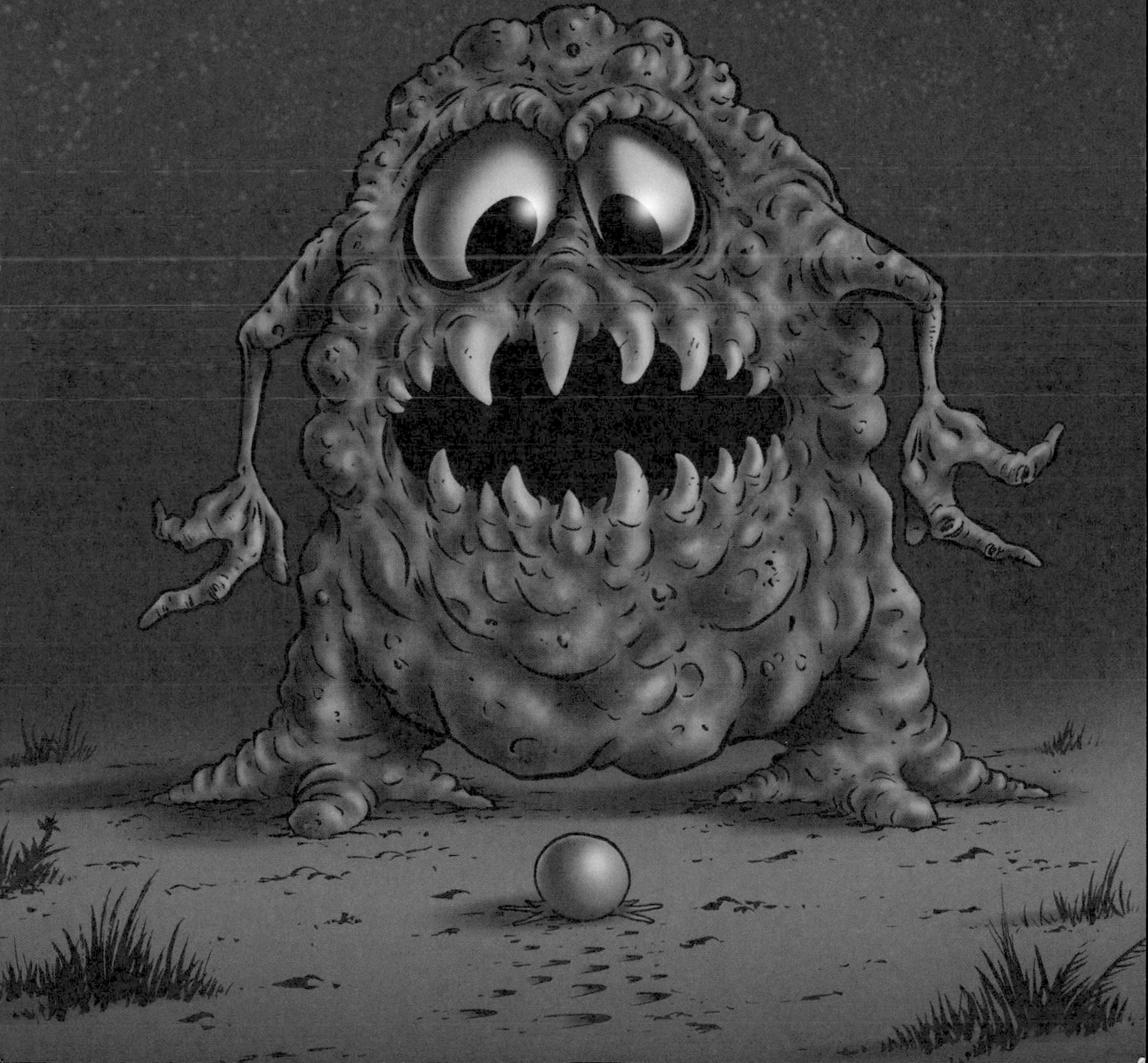

And the Colossux
opened his mouth
VERY WIDE...

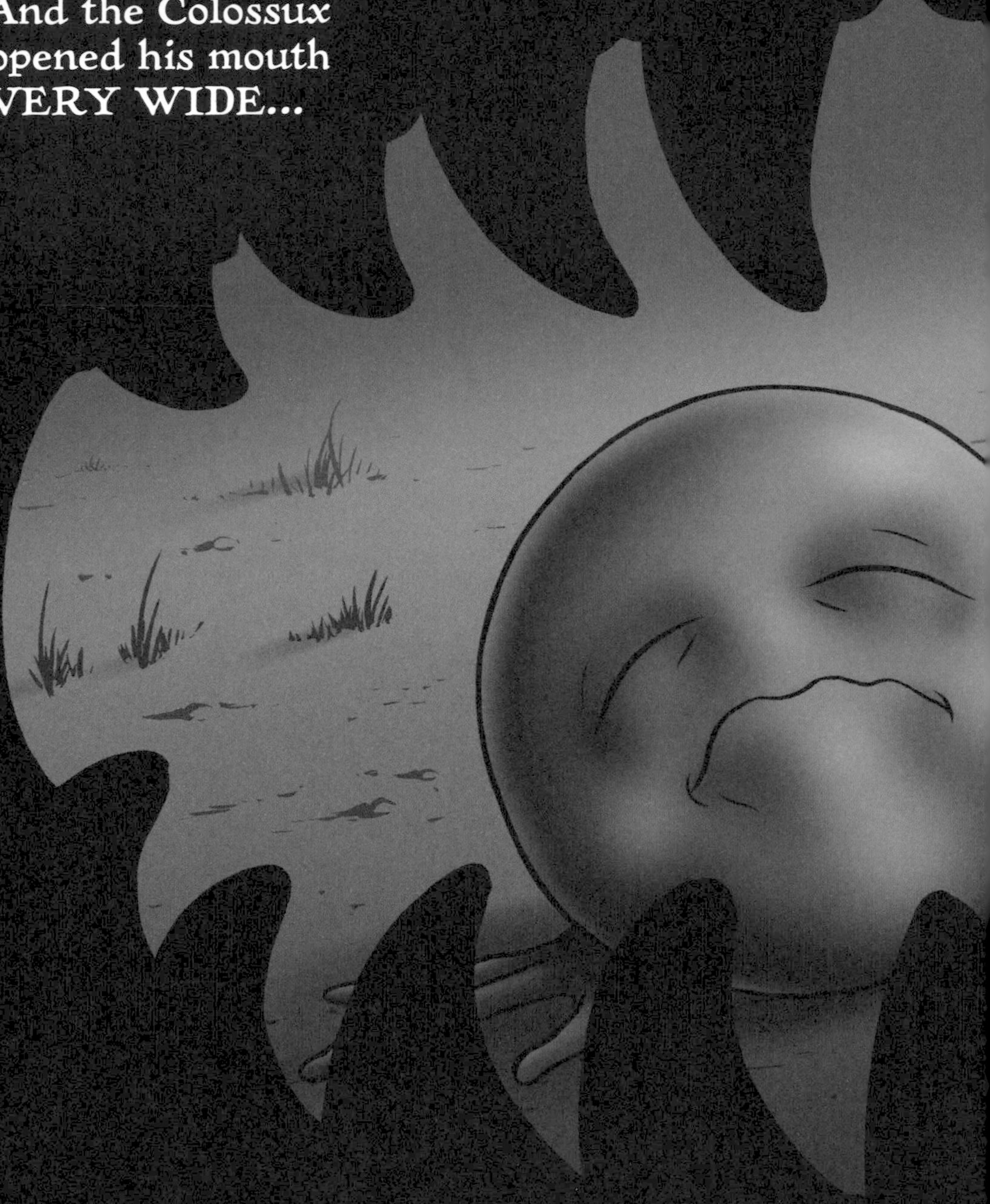

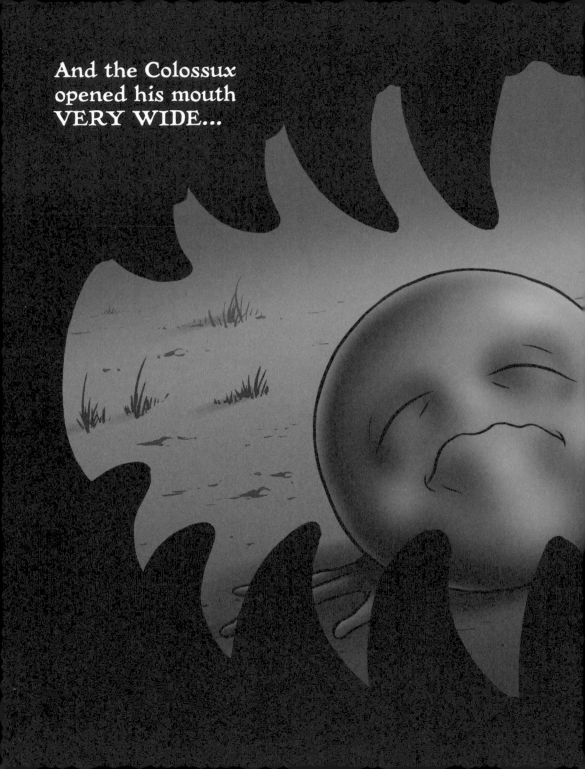

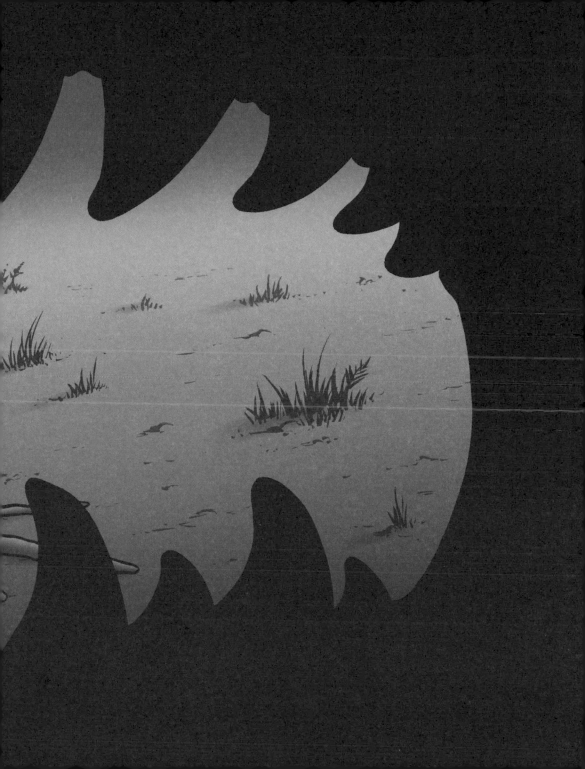

In the morning, Figwillop, The Booper
and KWAAH! woke up to find Erf gone.
They looked all over their new island,
but could find no sign of him.

All they could see...

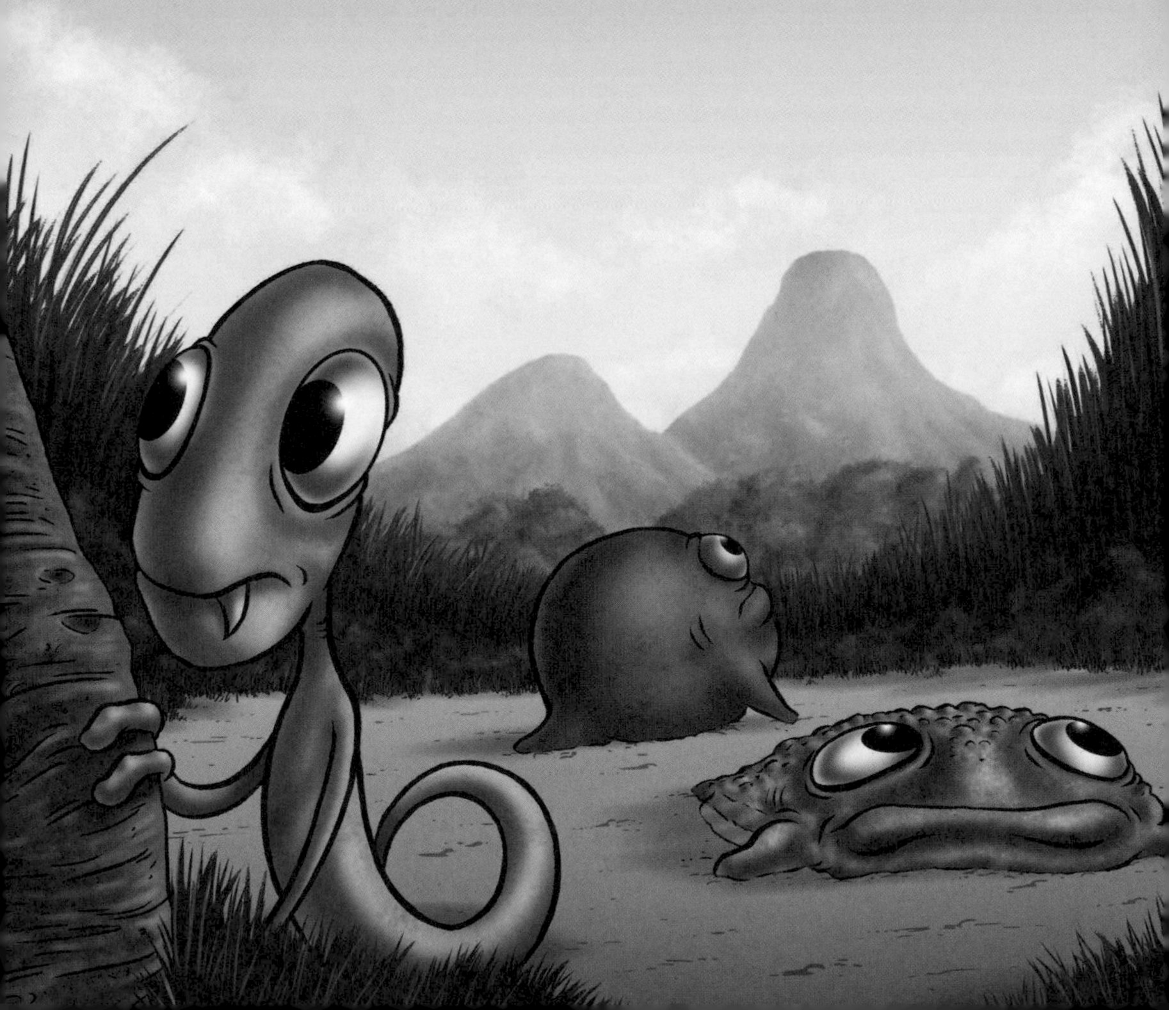

Was the Colossux, swimming away in the distance.

And that was when they knew Erf was gone.

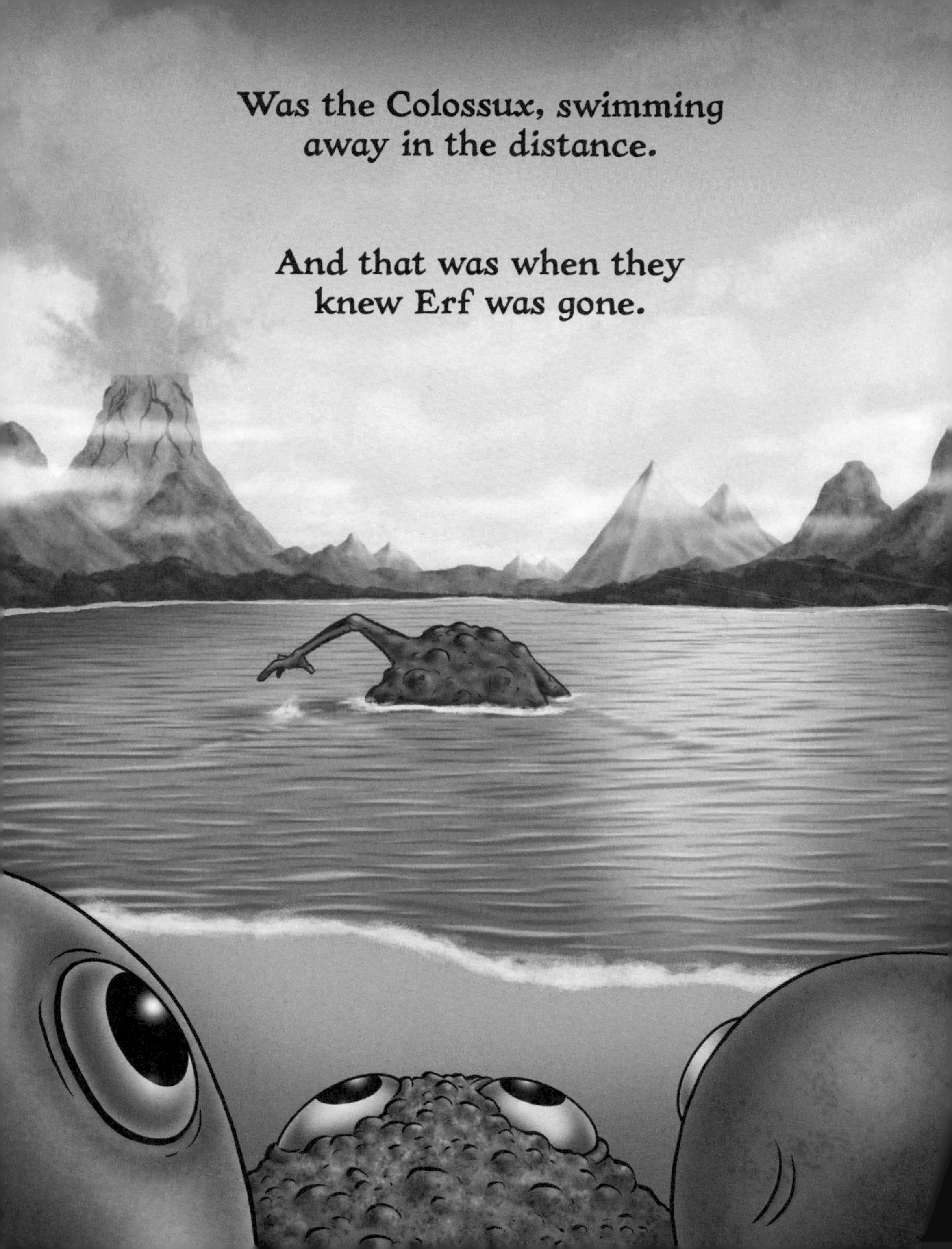

And they were very, very sad.

"It's all our fault," said Figwillop, "because we made Erf think we didn't need him."

"It's all our fault," said, The Booper, "because we didn't tell him we loved him enough."

"It's all our fault," said KWAAH! "because we didn't stand by our friend."

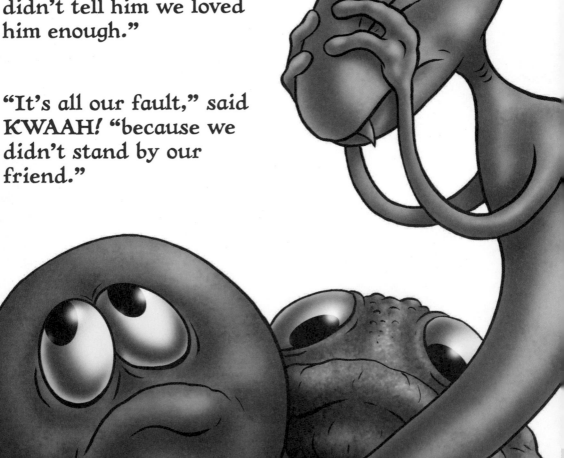

And then they understood that Erf did have a talent: he was very, very, very, very brave.

And now they had this wonderful world, but their friend wasn't there to enjoy it.

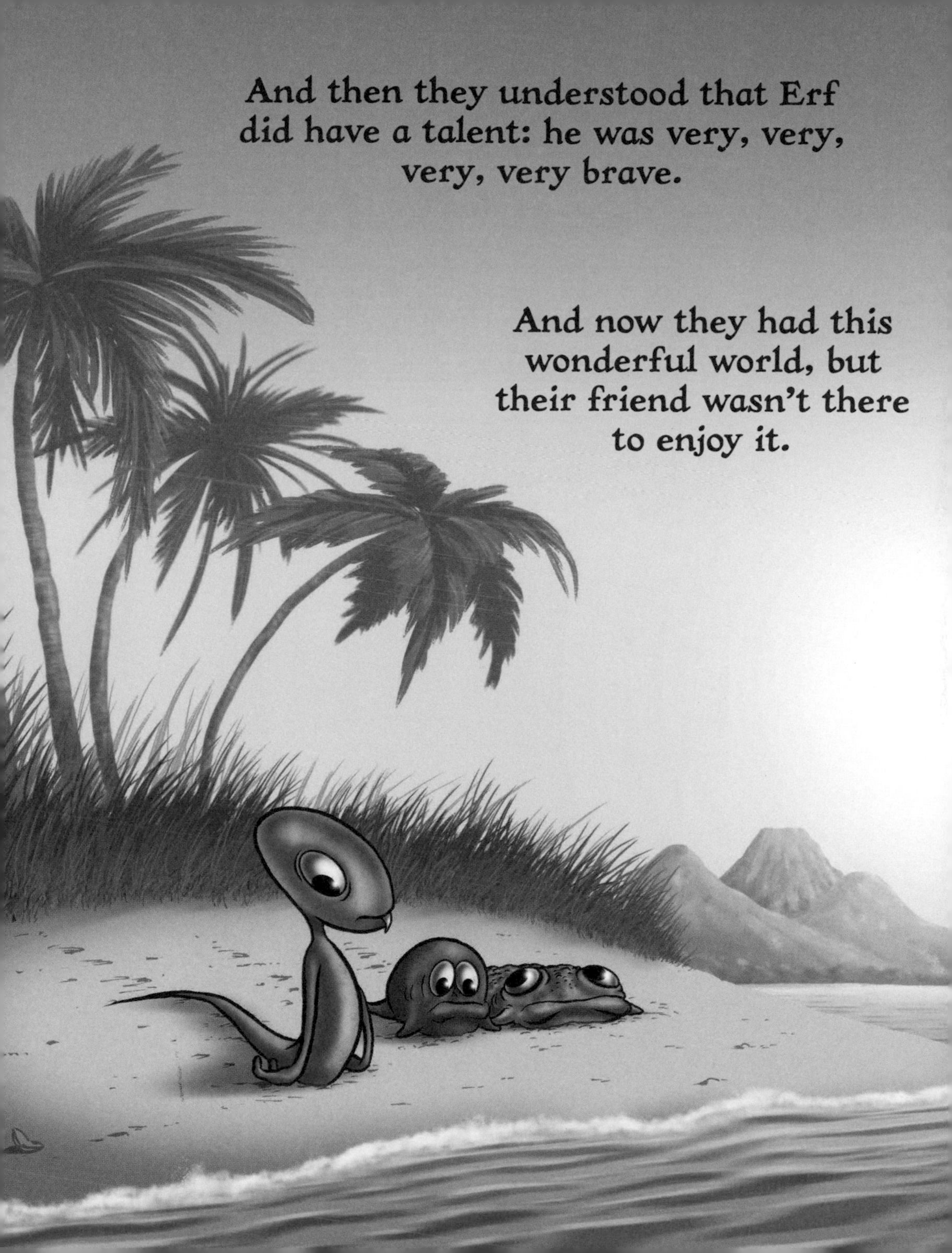

"Then we must never forget dear Erf," said Figwillop, and they made a promise, there and then.

"And we must always be true to each other," said The Booper, "so that his bravery wasn't in vain."

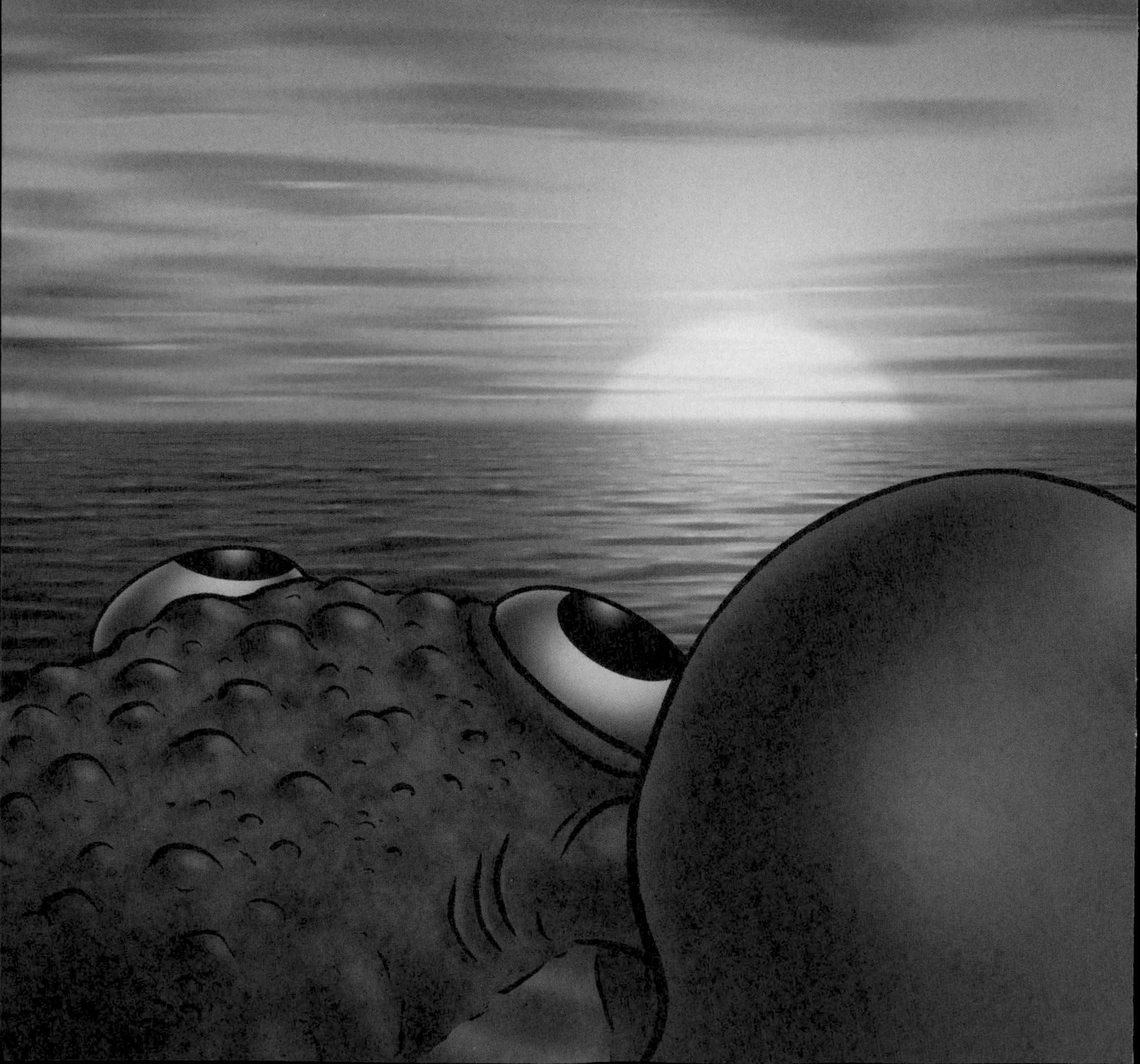

"And to honor him forever more," said KWAAH! "we shall name our new world after our friend."

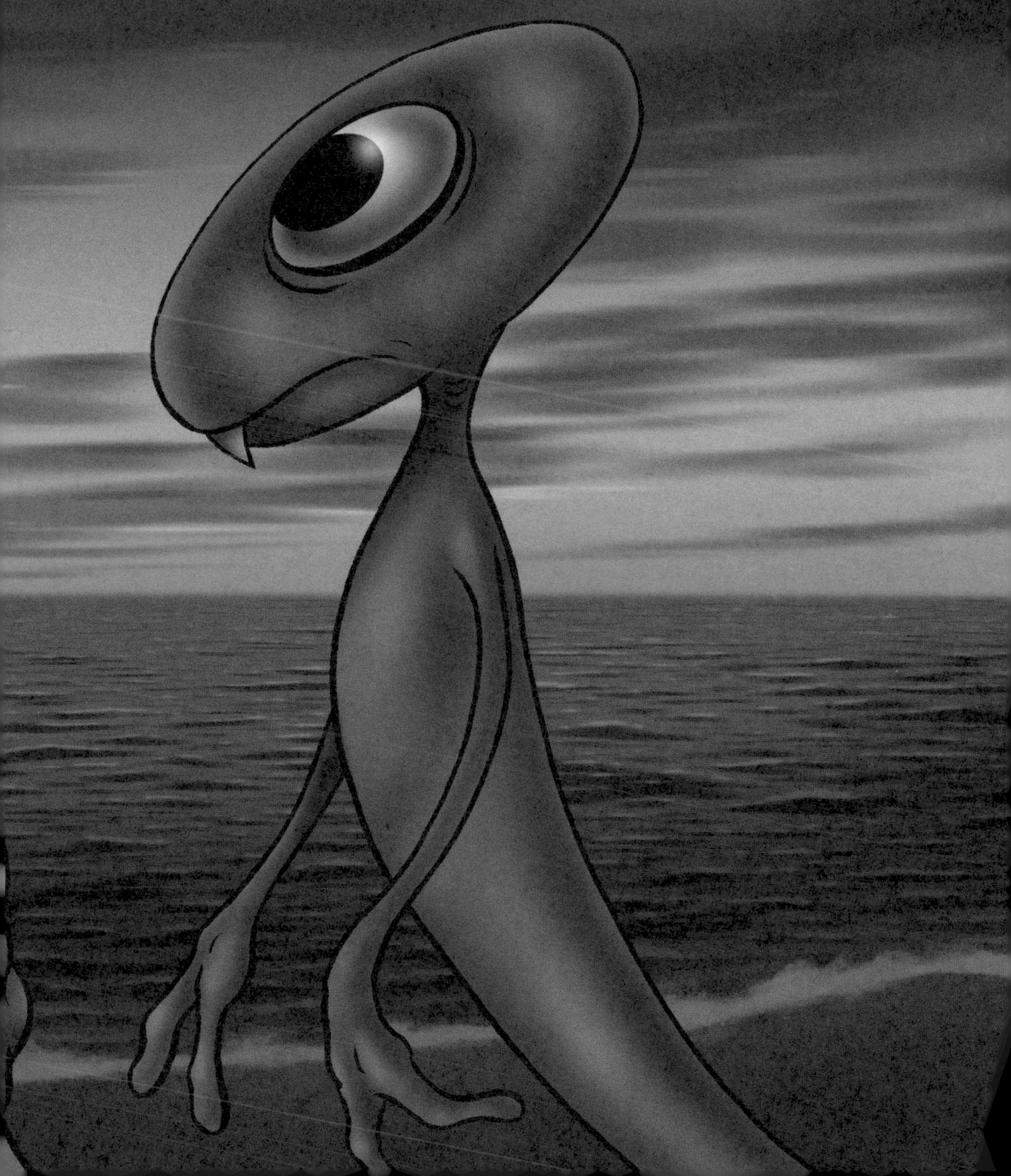

And they did.

And millions and millions and
millions and millions and millions and
millions of years went by.

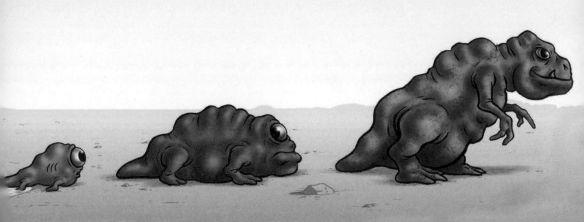

And the world became what
it is today, and eventually
WE came along.

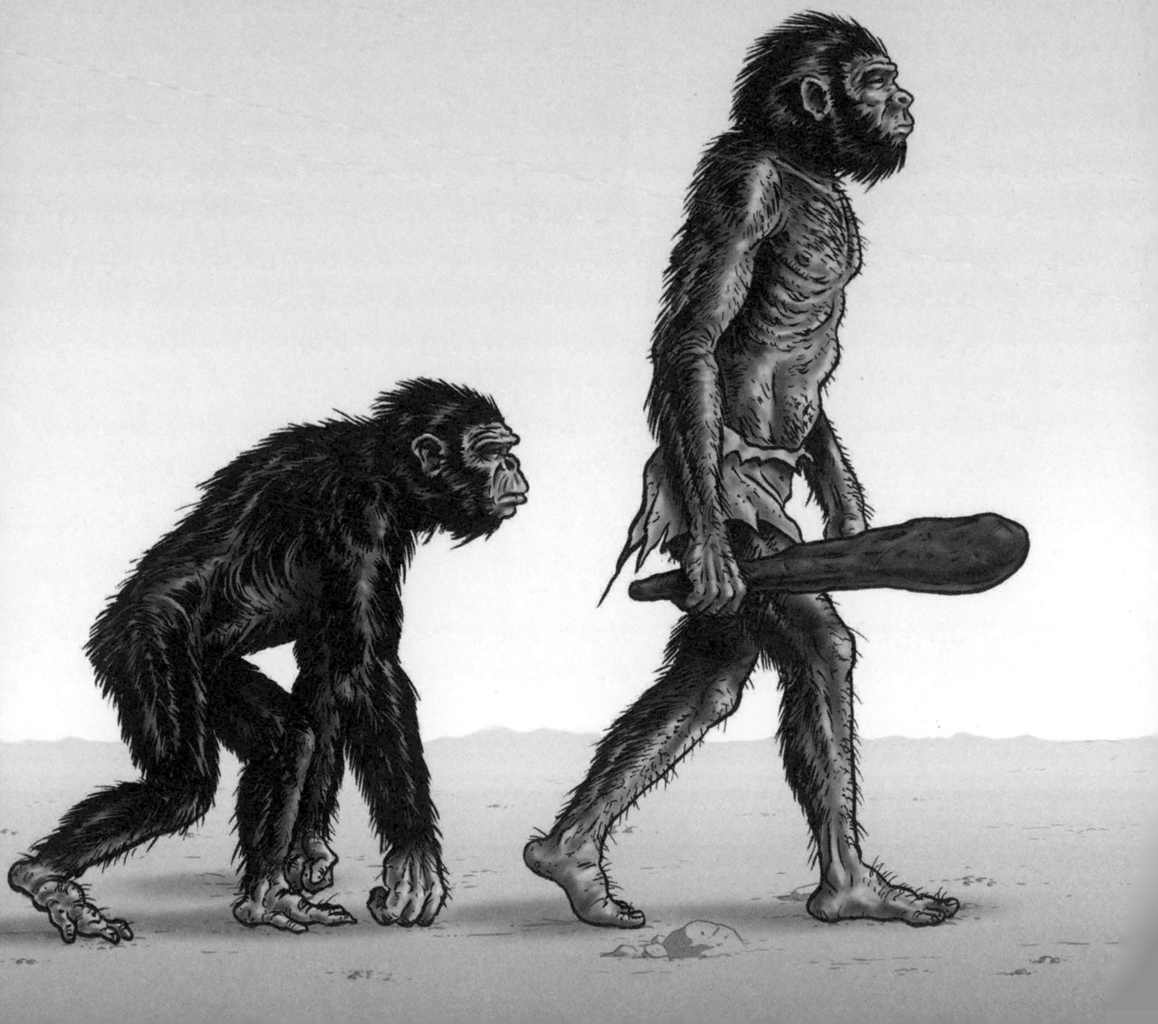

And once we got going, with our adventures
and inventions, and our cities and civilizations,
and all of our incredible dreams...

well, there was just no stopping us.

And even today...

After all those many millions of years...

Throughout all of the cities and civilizations...

The name that Figwillop, The Booper and KWAAH! gave to their new world...

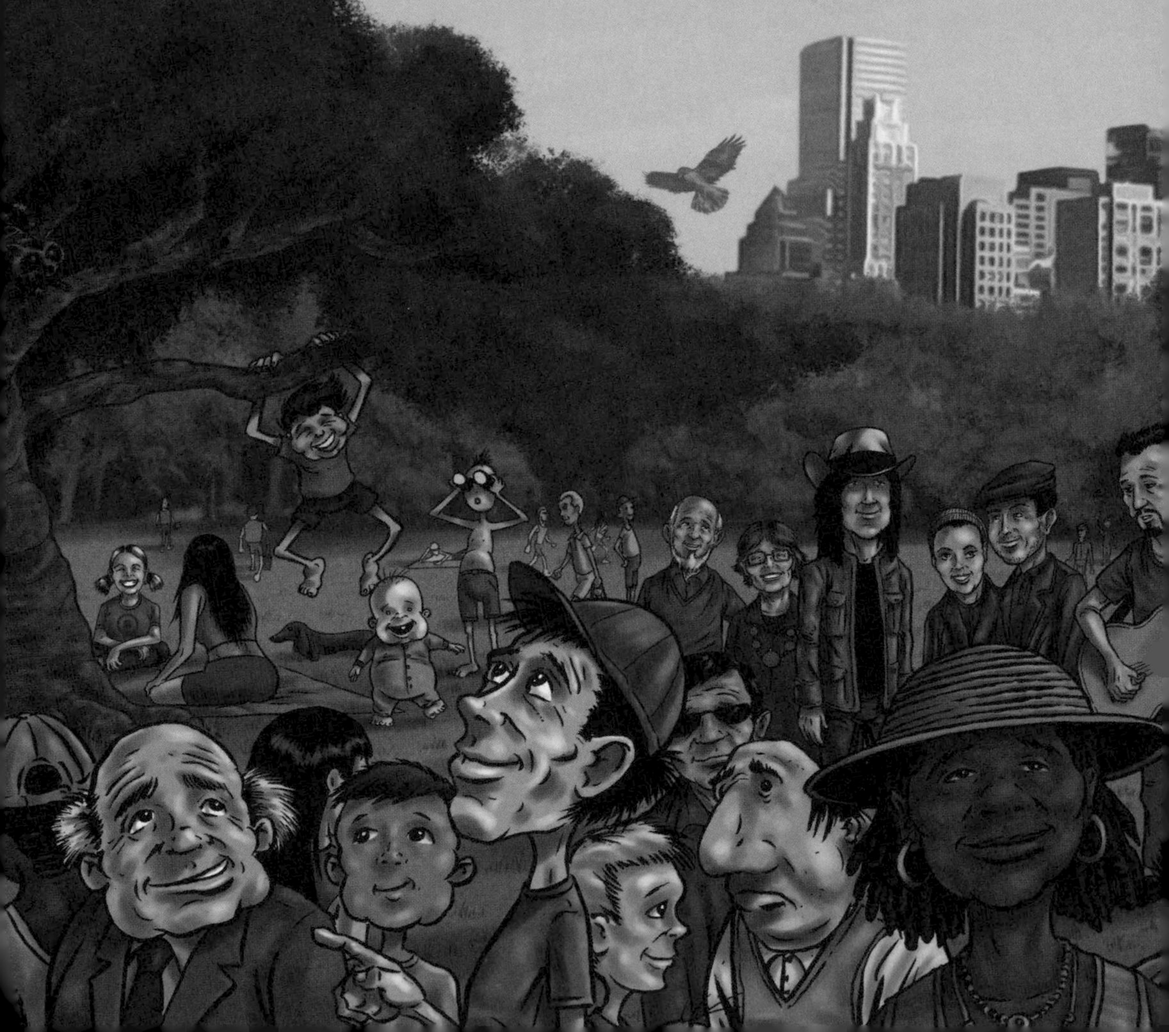

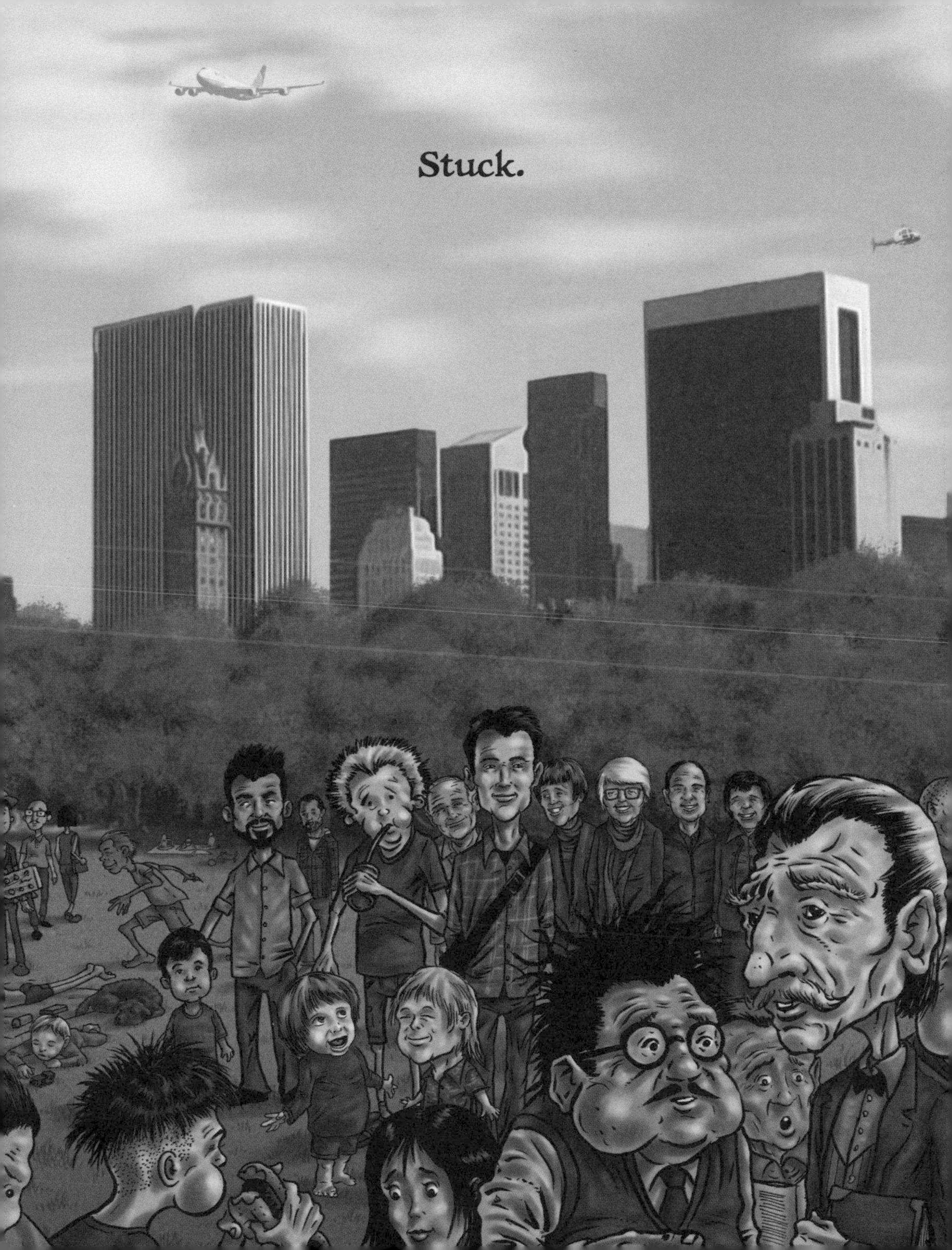
Stuck.

For who hasn't heard of Erf?

The End

Garth Ennis **is a British comic book writer living and working in New York. Best known for the Vertigo series** *Preacher,* **his other credits include** *The Boys, Battlefields, Crossed* **and a successful run on Marvel Comics'** *The Punisher.* **He has won the Eisner Award for Best Writer.**

Rob Steen **is the illustrator of the children's book series** *Flanimals,* **written by Ricky Gervais.** *Flanimals of the Deep* **won the Galaxy Award in the UK for Best Children's Book.**